Acknowledgements: With thanks to Steve and the boys at 'The Games Vault' for the brainstorming sessions. I never thought to find such a useful source of expertise on my doorstep.

SIMON AND SCHUSTER

First published in Great Britain by Simon and Schuster UK Ltd, 2009
A CBS COMPANY

Copyright © Mark Robson
Cover illustration by David Wyatt © 2009

3 5 7 9 10 8 6 4 2

Simon & Schuster UK Ltd
1st Floor
222 Gray's Inn Road
London WC1X 8HB

A CIP catalogue record for this book is
available from the British Library

ISBN 978-1-84738-070-8

Typeset by Rowland Phototypesetting Ltd,
Bury St Edmunds, Suffolk
Printed and bound in Great Britain by
CPI Group (UK) Ltd, Croydon, CR0 4YY

For Justin,
Wishing you happiness and a dream that
will inspire you to great things.

Also by Mark Robson

Dragon Orb 1: Firestorm
Dragon Orb 2: Shadow

Imperial Spy
Imperial Assassin
Imperial Traitor

For information on future
books and other stories
by Mark Robson, visit:
www.markrobsonauthor.com

Contents

Chapter One
Out of the Valley

Ever protected, the dusk orb lies
Behind the cover, yet no disguise.
Afterlife image, unreal yet real,
Lives in the shadows, waits to reveal.

Pell clutched at his left shoulder as the searing pain took his breath away. Flare after flare of mind-numbing agony lanced through the telepathic bond he shared with his night dragon, Shadow, and tears welled in his eyes.

The wound to his dragon was serious. She was losing blood fast. It was a tough decision, but he knew that to escape the Valley of the Griffins with the dark orb intact, his best chance was to have Shadow's wound seared shut with dragonfire.

It seemed incredible that it was only two weeks

1

since Pell and his three companions Elian, Kira and Nolita, had met with the Oracle, a spirit creature revered by dragons all over Areth. At the Oracle's command, the Great Quest for the four dragon orbs had begun. Pell was still not totally convinced that Elian, Kira and Nolita were being honest with him. He had set off alone to seek the dark orb of the night dragons while the others went off in pursuit of the day orb. Betrayed and imprisoned by Segun, leader of the night dragon enclave, Pell had almost lost hope of completing his mission. To his embarrassment and relief, the others had come to his rescue. But they told an improbable tale of Nolita gaining the day orb and delivering it to the Oracle. He pretended to accept what they told him, but secretly he had serious doubts about it.

Winning the dark orb had been both difficult and costly. Griffins guarded the valley where the orb was hidden. When Pell arrived there, the senior council of the night dragons, led by Segun, had got there first. The harsh-voiced speaker of the griffins, Karrok, insisted that a champion from each party should compete for the honour of 'revealing' the orb. Each wave of heat that now surged through Pell's shoulder triggered memories of that struggle. Segun had delegated Dirk, an immensely strong dragonrider, to represent the night dragon enclave and compete against Pell. During the final challenge, Dirk's dragon, Knifetail, had dealt Shadow the slashing blow to her shoulder that had opened the deep wound.

A low, rumbling roar reverberated around the valley basin, as Firestorm, Nolita's day dragon, now breathed his hottest flames in a controlled jet over the gaping gash in Shadow's shoulder. Burning pain flooded across the mental bridge that linked Pell to his dragon, and his own shoulder burned in sympathy. He gripped it and squeezed hard to try to convince his body that it was not his own flesh that was melting. The pain contrasted with the icy stab of defeat he had felt a few minutes earlier, when Dirk had beaten him to the orb. If the griffins had not seen Pell's opponent cheat to win, Segun would have taken possession of the orb and destroyed it. The night dragon leader was willing to do anything to see Pell and his companions fail, thereby ensuring the Oracle's death and freeing him to declare supremacy over all dragonkind.

To complete his part of the Oracle's quest, Pell had to return the dark orb to the Dragon Spirit in the mountains of Orupee. The way things were going the worst might yet be still to come. He had defied Segun, and the leader of the night dragon enclave was not the sort to forgive and forget.

'This quest had better be worth it,' Pell groaned through gritted teeth. 'First outlawed by my dragon enclave. Now this.'

The telepathic link between dragon and rider brought many benefits, but this time Pell wished there was a way of shutting off the flow of thoughts and feelings. The roar of flame stopped, but the pain barely dimmed. He dashed the tears from his eyes with the back of his hand and ran forwards through the snow to inspect Shadow's wound as Firestorm stepped back. It wasn't pretty, but it had stopped bleeding.

'Fire says it's the best he can do.' Nolita's voice at Pell's shoulder startled him. He had not realised she was there. Nolita did not come close to dragons unless she had to, as they terrified her. The irony that one so scared of large animals should be a dragonrider was not lost on Pell, who felt that her cowardice reflected badly on all dragonriders. As yet, he had seen nothing to change that opinion, but he knew he had to work with her. Her dragon had abilities that were useful to his cause. 'He's genuinely sorry that his healing fire won't work on night dragons,' Nolita said.

'I'm sure he is,' Pell grunted. No sooner had the words left his mouth than he realised how ungrateful they sounded. He turned to face her and saw the hurt in her eyes. 'Sorry, Nolita, that didn't come out the way I intended. Please pass my thanks to Firestorm. I'm sure he did what he could. We'll be fine. Shadow's strong.'

'Yes,' she said, as her haunted eyes rose to meet those of the huge black dragon. 'She is.'

Nolita backed away slowly, as Shadow proceeded to roll gently onto her side and dip the smoking wound into the deep snow. There was a hiss and a small cloud of steam rose around her shoulder. The sympathetic pain in Pell's shoulder lessened considerably.

Elian and Kira intercepted Nolita before she had moved more than a few paces.

'We need to get out of here while we can,' Kira urged, looking first to where Longfang, her dusk dragon, stood waiting and then up at the dozens of vicious-looking griffins circling overhead. 'The griffins promised to stop Segun and the others from following us until sunset, but that only gives us a couple of hours at best. Segun is furious. Once the griffins let him leave, he'll stop at nothing to destroy the dark orb.'

'The other three night dragons are also out there somewhere,' Elian, the rider of dawn dragon, Aurora, added. 'Ra tells me the weather's on the turn. Things could get rough, but if we can hold out

5

until dawn, she can get all of us out of this mess.'

'And into another most likely,' Kira muttered.

Pell felt Shadow getting back to her feet behind him. The cold snow must have soothed her pain, as the burning sensation in Pell's shoulder had diminished to a dull throbbing. 'In case you hadn't noticed, things are already rough,' he growled. 'But you're right. We need to go. It's a long way to the Oracle's cave.'

As he spoke, Pell caught sight of Segun. The tall rider wore a sadistic expression of pleasure at the sight of Pell's obvious pain. A sudden urge to race across and wipe the smile from Segun's face made Pell's right hand go instinctively for his knife. Segun's eyes followed Pell's hand and the night dragon leader's cruel smile broadened further. The man was vicious. Pell had watched him kill one of his own lieutenants a few minutes earlier. The leader of the night dragon riders had not shown so much as a flicker of remorse afterwards. Common sense crushed Pell's rash impulse. He whirled round and bounded up Shadow's side, twisting neatly into the saddle and slotting his booted feet into the stirrups.

'*Are you ready to fly again?*' he asked Shadow through their mental link.

'*We have what we came for,*' she replied. '*I am as*

ready as I'm going to be. Let us show Segun that it will take more than a bit of pain to stop us.'

Kira looked around as her dragon, Longfang, turned to face down the valley towards the exit tunnel. The others were mounted and ready to go. She saw Pell give an impudent salute in the direction of Segun and his dragon, Widewing. Frustration and anger boiled inside her. Was the boy a complete fool? Baiting a lion was an act of stupidity that had inevitable consequences. Even the youngest child in her tribe knew that. Taunting Segun was worse. And Pell thought himself to be the natural leader for the quest! Kira ground her teeth as the older boy gave the word to his dragon, Shadow. The huge night dragon sprang forwards into her take-off run.

'*Come on, Fang,*' Kira said, unable to keep her frustration from colouring her tone. '*We'd better follow them before they get themselves into more trouble.*'

As they accelerated it was hard to ignore the huge red area of blood-soaked snow and the lifeless carcass of the night dragon, Knifetail. Her twisted body had been literally torn open by griffins, and her heart now formed the centre of the dark orb tucked deep in Pell's saddlebag. Kira shuddered. The body could so easily have been that of Shadow,

7

but Dirk, Pell's opponent in the challenge for the dark orb, had cheated and inadvertently brought the fate upon his own dragon. For the briefest moment, the thought crossed Kira's mind that their quest might have stood more chance of success if it *had* been Shadow who had died. Pell and Shadow had done nothing but lead them into trouble by trying to act alone since the quest began.

That's unkind thinking, Kira, she berated herself. Pell is annoying, but the Oracle chose him in the same way it chose me. He and Nolita have won their orbs and both went through painful trials to get them. It's my turn next. What if the dusk orb also requires a dark sacrifice? Will *I* do whatever it takes to see the Oracle survive?

The question hung in her mind, but she could not bring herself to answer it. She had no answer. How could she say without knowing what price she might have to pay?

Let's get the dark orb to the Oracle, she thought. There'll be time to worry about the dusk orb later.

Longfang skipped into the air and Kira was forced to concentrate on the take off. Ahead, she saw Shadow's wings kicking vortices of snow into the air. She glanced across at Fang's wingtips. He too was stirring up mini-whirlwinds that swirled white against the vertical rock walls on either side of the deep mountain valley. They fizzled out quite quickly, but Kira had never seen anything like them before. They were fascinating.

She realised her focus had slipped again. Why was she getting distracted so easily? This was not like her. If anything, she should be working on practical considerations. She needed to plan their next move. Even with one dragon and his rider dead, Segun still held the advantage of numbers. He and his four remaining lieutenants would undoubtedly mount their night dragons and give chase as soon as the griffins allowed them to leave at sunset, and there were three more riders on night dragons waiting for them somewhere outside the valley. If Segun joined forces with them, he would outnumber the questors by two to one. Not good odds, but Kira knew that if they could hold off the night dragons until dawn, Aurora could open a gateway into the other world, where Segun and his men could not follow them. Despite the strangeness and the horrors of war that awaited them there, Kira felt certain that going through the gateway would solve many of their immediate problems.

The valley narrowed until they reached the sharp right turn into the tunnel that led out of the Valley of the Griffins. The familiar pressure forced her down hard against Fang's back as he tipped into a steep turn. The rock walls to either side raced past as they rolled back to level flight. Looking ahead, Kira could see the end of the tunnel beyond Shadow and Pell. Spots of white were visible in the air. Snow was beginning to fall.

'Fang, do you see what I see?' she asked.

'Yes, it's snowing,' he replied. 'But don't worry. This could prove to be the best luck we've had all day.'

'Luck? In what way?'

'Visibility will be limited, but it will be far easier to throw Segun off our trail.'

'Well I'm glad there's something good about it,' Kira said sourly. 'We're going to get extremely cold and wet, and I've had quite enough of the cold. I hope the dusk orb is somewhere warmer.'

'Shadow will probably welcome the cold and wet after Firestorm sealed her wound with his fire,' Fang pointed out. 'She is strong, but that's a nasty wound she's taken. I know I would not be able to fly far with the pain she is suffering. Keeping the cauterised area cool will help to ease it a little. Night dragons are not easily harmed. Unfortunately, they do not heal easily either. I imagine it will be some years before she'll be free from the pain of that injury.'

'Years! But that's awful! And Pell will feel her pain all that time?' The part of her that disliked Pell wanted to take sadistic pleasure in that thought, but she knew what it had felt like when Fang had been injured by dragonhunters.

'*Don't worry, Kira,*' Fang answered. '*Pell may be annoying, but he is strong. Shadow is strong too. They will recover.*'

The icy breeze as they emerged from the end of the tunnel cut through Kira's protective clothing as if it were made of thin Racafian cloth. Although snow was falling, it was still light, and the visibility along the valley was not too bad. Kira could see the best part of a league in both directions, but a quick glance at the cloud above was enough for her to realise it would not stay this benign for long.

'*Shadow is suggesting we head southwards, but stay amongst the peaks until it starts to get dark,*' Fang told her. '*In these conditions I'd normally want to get out of the mountains as quickly as possible, but that would leave us vulnerable to attack. Remaining in the network of valleys while it is snowing will bring danger, but it will make it far more difficult for Segun and his men to find us. I think Shadow's plan is probably sensible.*'

They turned right along the valley and on reaching the first fork they turned left. Pell had told them about his final race for the orb. This valley took them away from the race route. More importantly, it took them away from the last place Pell had seen one of the three night dragons they knew to be lurking in the mountain range.

The mountain peaks slipped past on either side as the dragons did their best to fly at high speed, but they had not gone far when the snowflakes began to get bigger and more numerous. The wind picked up, moaning and howling across rocks and hollows on the steep slopes. Visibility worsened and the air became rough with turbulence as the mountainous slopes twisted its flow, shaping it into swirling vortices and wicked vertical drafts.

'This is not good. If it gets any worse, I think we might have to land somewhere and try to hide away until dawn.' Fang's voice in Kira's mind sounded worried. They had hardly gone any distance from the Valley of the Griffins. If the blizzard conditions blew through before dusk, it would leave Segun and his men almost on top of them.

'I don't like it,' Kira said. *'We need to get further away.'*

'I agree that would be ideal, but if this gets any worse it will become impossible to see where we're going. My eyesight is the best amongst the dragons and I'm struggling to see far enough ahead to fly safely. How Shadow is leading the way in this, I don't know.'

'Then let's try to get clear of the mountains and fly in the open air to the east of here,' Kira suggested. *'We*

can parallel the range southwards and then nip back in among the peaks to hide when it becomes necessary.'

'That sounds like a good compromise,' Fang agreed. 'Assuming we can get that far without crashing blindly into a mountainside. I'll put it to Shadow and see what she says.'

Kira could see very little now. Her eyes were almost shut in an effort to keep out the driving snow. She looked first to one side and then the other, squinting and straining in an effort to see her companions. Every now and then she caught a glimpse of one of them before the falling curtain of white snow swallowed them again. She knew Fang was right. Continuing to fly in these conditions was madness, but if they were to stand a realistic chance of escaping Segun's reach, they had to press on.

Her face began to go numb with cold as the icy flakes leeched the heat from her flesh. Glancing down she found her jacket and the front of her trousers were white with snow. More was accumulating on the front of Fang's ridges and the leading edges of his wings. As the cloud was thickening and the snowfall intensifying, so the light levels were dropping. It felt almost like dusk, though the sun would not set for some time yet.

'I cannot say I'm happy,' Fang reported. 'But the consensus amongst the dragons is to press on and try to get clear of the mountains. *We must hope for the conditions to improve. It will be less dangerous once we are out of the range. Shadow is going to descend to see if the visibility is better lower down. I've agreed to try climbing. Hold on tight. This is likely to get very uncomfortable.'*

Kira did as she was told, leaning as flat as she could against Fang's back in an effort to minimise the biting cold of the wind and snow cutting through her jacket. The temperature would get colder as they climbed and Kira already felt as if the seat of her trousers was frozen to her saddle.

Fang had barely begun his climb when the spine-chilling screech of a night dragon rent the air. For a horrible moment Kira imagined that Shadow had crashed into the ground, but then she realised the sound had not come from below them, but from behind. And it was close. Very close. They were under attack.

Chapter Two
The Dark Orb

Pell gripped the pommel as tightly as he could as Shadow dropped with a stomach-turning lurch. As they dived, he found his eyes began to play tricks on him. Unless he looked specifically at something nearby, like one of Shadow's ridges, or a wing, his focus shifted, unable to settle on anything. This made his eyes hurt as if he were deliberately crossing and uncrossing them.

A distant screech rent the air. It was a dragon's cry and it came from somewhere above them. Pell's chest tightened. He knew the voices of his companions' dragons well enough to know that the cry was not one of theirs. It was the cry of a night dragon. Another voice replied, this time from ahead. Their enemies had laid an ambush. And he had led his companions right into it.

The night dragons were closing. Pell could almost feel their proximity. His skin crawled with the anticipation of an imminent attack. As Shadow dived lower and lower, he scanned the swirling curtain of snow overhead for any sign of incoming dragons. Where were his companions? Had they already been attacked?

'The others scattered,' Shadow said, her voice calming. 'We will try to meet up later some way south of here. The night dragons should leave them alone. It's us they are really after – us, and the orb. The snow should work in our favour, though. Barring accidents, or blind chance, the blizzard will make it impossible for the night dragons to coordinate an effective pursuit.'

'But what if they—'

'Don't start with the "what ifs", Pell,' Shadow interrupted firmly. 'Let's concentrate on getting ourselves out of here. The others can look after themselves.'

Chastened, Pell clung tightly to the pommel as they levelled out from their shallow dive and skimmed across the smooth white surface of the snow-filled valley basin. The wind picked up fast as the snowstorm struck with its full fury. Flurries of snow whipped up from the ground, racing on the wind in dense white rolls of cloudlike foaming waves on a storm-tossed sea, mixing and whirling with the myriad flakes falling from above. He felt helpless. It was all up to Shadow again.

The icy blast of the bitter wind cut through his clothing and his face began to sting as the large flakes suddenly changed into pellets of soft hail. Shadow hugged the contours of the valley floor, staying as low as she dared. Weaving and bumping, she threaded her way along the valley, manoeuvring her gigantic frame like a dragon half her size.

'Try to watch our backs,' she warned. 'It's taking all my focus to keep us from hitting the ground. I can't watch for incoming dragons as well.'

The responsibility of watching the sky for enemies was just what Pell needed. It gave him a sense of purpose that warmed him inside and set his mind alight.

'I'll do my best,' he told her, though he quickly realised that his best was not very good. It was impossible to see much at all.

'I think we're nearly through the worst of it,' she warned. 'As soon as visibility begins to improve, we'll become more vulnerable to attack. Stay alert.'

Pell could feel Shadow's shoulder burning with pain again. Not with the heat of Firestorm's flame, but with the fatigue that comes from pushing muscles too hard. They had not flown far from the

Valley of the Griffins, but they had completed an exhausting series of flying challenges before they left. Shadow's injury was well forwards of her wings but, with the pain as a reference, Pell could trace the interaction of the muscles in her body through the bond. The combination of fatigue and her injury meant that every beat of her wings now carried a penalty spike of pain that was slowly building in intensity. She was brave, but he could feel her weakening. She was strong enough and stubborn enough to keep flying for some time yet, but at what cost?

'I'm sorry, Shadow, but it's no good. We're going to have to land,' Pell told her, his mind made up. *'My hands are numb. I can't hold on much longer. Try to find the deepest snowdrift you can. Set us down and I'll do my best to camouflage you with snow. If it keeps falling at this rate for even a short while longer, then the weather will complete what I can't.'*

There was a pause as Shadow considered his suggestion. Pell did not know if she could see through his lie, but he was confident she would know he had her best interests at heart.

'Very well,' she replied reluctantly. *'I'll see what I can do.'*

The wind flow was generally westerly, so Shadow eased across to the eastern side of the valley, where

18

the snow was drifting deepest. Picking her spot, she landed, limping to an awkward stop as the tricky wind conditions made it impossible to touch down gently. Pell looked down and saw that the snow was barely deeper than her talons. It was certainly nowhere near deep enough to bury her.

'This won't do,' he told her. 'The snow looked deeper from the air.'

'On the lee side of some of the bigger rocks there are drifts up to a couple of spans deep,' she replied. 'Look over here.' The dragon stepped gingerly across to the grey face of a huge boulder, folding her wings tight against her sides as she went. The closer she got, the deeper the snow became. 'You had better get down and take your saddlebags. They might be difficult to get at in a minute.'

A screech sounded high overhead. It made Pell jump. He looked up, but he could see nothing. Moving as quickly as his cold fingers would allow, he did as he was told. It was hard to unbuckle the saddlebags, but he managed it. The first, he threw down. It landed with a *whumpf* in the soft snow. The second, which contained the orb, he held in his arms as he slid down Shadow's side. He landed heavily, sinking almost knee deep into the white powder. It was deep, but not heavy. The flakes falling now were large and quite wet, but the main depth already on the ground was formed of fine particles of snow that parted easily, almost fizzing around his legs as he started to wade through it.

No sooner had he moved clear of her side than Shadow stepped forwards, pushing into the much deeper snow behind the gigantic rock and easing the bulk of her body behind it in a great semi-circle. She curled her tail tight in to the front rock face and wrapped her head and long neck around to meet her tail. Although her purple-black colouring was not a great match with the dark grey rock, as the sun set and the snow continued to cover her up, her body shape would become progressively harder to pick out from the air.

'Are you comfortable there, Shadow?' Pell asked.

'Surprisingly comfortable,' she replied. 'The snow on my wound is most soothing.'

'That's great. Now stay still,' he told her. 'I'm just going to break up your outline a bit and then we'll wait for dark. Once the sun's gone down, we'll search for the others. It'll be far safer to move under cover of darkness.'

'If we were anywhere else in the world, I would agree with you,' she said, her voice carrying more than a hint of doubt. 'But the short period of darkness here will not bring the safety it might elsewhere. My black scales will stand out against the white of the snow by day or night. Even the slightest starlight will be enough to make me conspicuous from above. When we move, we'll have to climb quickly if we're to avoid Segun's men spotting us.'

She was right, but there was no time to worry about that now. The snow was coming down so hard, it was already beginning to mottle her back, which was great, but not good enough to hide her. Pell had to work fast to camouflage her effectively.

Placing the saddlebags by the dark rock face, he waded around to the base of Shadow's back where he began to scoop up armload after armload of snow and throw it over her body. His intention was to break up her shape, so that anyone looking from the air would not see the obvious outline of a dragon. Creating an uneven path of white across her back did not take long and the vigorous exercise warmed him. As soon as he was content that he had effectively severed Shadow's tail with a broad path of white, he moved in front of the enormous rock and repeated the exercise at her neck.

'What will you do when you've finished, Pell?' she asked him as he threw more and more snow over her. 'Where will you rest? There's not much cover here.'

'Don't worry about me,' he replied. 'I'll dig a hole into the side of the big drift behind you and wait out the storm there. I've holed up in a snow bank before. It's actually quite comfortable once you're in it.'

A few more minutes of frantic shovelling with his arms and Pell knew he had done all he could realistically do to camouflage his dragon. The cold would not harm her, so he began working on digging himself a shelter. The wind was howling now and the temperature was dropping fast as the big flakes and snow pellets gave way to the much finer crystalline flakes that formed the body of the snow around him. Driven by the wind, the fine flakes pricked his skin constantly like a million tiny needles and soon he could no longer tell the difference between hot and cold.

It took a few minutes of digging before he realised his plan held a serious flaw. The powdery snow was great for throwing over Shadow's back, but it was so fine and loose that burrowing a safe hole into the side of the drift was impossible. Every time he began to get any way into the bank, the roof of his hole collapsed. Within a few minutes he saw it was hopeless. Even if he did manage to dig a hole of suitable size and depth, it was likely to cave in on him. The thought of suffocating under the snow was not a pleasant one.

'Looks like I'm going to need a new plan,' he muttered aloud as he abandoned his efforts at digging. He paused for a moment to think, and then he turned to address his dragon. '*Can you ease your*

head away from the rock a little, Shadow? I'm going to
squeeze into the gap to keep out of the wind. Sunset can't
be much more than an hour away now. We'll move
again then.'

Shadow was happy to oblige. She shifted her
head and Pell squeezed into the hollow, pulling
his saddlebags in behind him. He sighed with relief
as he crouched down. It felt fantastic to be out
of the wind and for a moment he just squatted
there, listening to its cruel howling voice. In the
comparative stillness of his shelter, he began to feel
a gentle burning sensation in his ears, cheeks and
fingers, as blood began to work its way back into
his extremities. Although the renewed circulation
brought pain, it was nothing like the deep burning
of Firestorm's blazing breath earlier. This heat in his
flesh felt wholesome and almost pleasurable.

Fumbling through his saddlebags, Pell pulled out
his spare cloak and wrapped it over his head and
around his shoulders like a shawl. The material was
soft and thick, bringing a further sense of comfort
and protection. Tucked up against Shadow's cheek,
he felt safe both from the elements and from the
pursuing dragons. He listened long and hard, but he
heard nothing apart from the wind. If the night
dragons were still above them, they were no longer
calling to one another.

How long it was before he began to feel the pull of the orb, Pell did not know. The urge to get it out was subtle at first, beginning with daydreams – flashbacks of how he had attained the orb and then images of how it felt in his hands. The images were twisted. As he daydreamed, he felt a shock of pleasure every time he pictured himself holding the orb, yet in the back of his mind the truth haunted him like a nightmare. The aura of the orb had been colder than any snowstorm. He had not been able to dump the thing into his saddlebag fast enough. He had certainly not held it with bare hands, as the images in his mind portrayed.

Slowly, but surely, the desire to draw out the orb grew. Teasing. Tantalising. Taunting. His natural instinct was to resist, though he had no idea why. Eventually, however, the pull became less subtle and too strong for him to ignore. A sour taste formed in Pell's mouth as he looked down at the saddlebag containing the orb. It was open in front of him, but he had no conscious memory of having undone the straps. Tiny wisps of mist curled from the open top. His sight dimmed as he tried to remember the last few minutes and his heart rate accelerated as he sensed a dark cloud in his mind. A palpable aura pulsed inside the bag as if the orb were alive.

'*Shadow!*' he gasped, straining to prevent his hands moving towards the bag of their own volition.

'*I see them,*' she replied. '*Don't panic. There are a lot of them, but most of the animals are completely harmless. What do you think brought them here? They are acting very strangely. I've never known animals deliberately come anywhere near me before.*'

'*Animals? What are you talking about?*' he asked. 'It's the orb, Shadow! It's doing something to me. I . . . can't . . . stop . . .'

'*I feel it now. Sorry, Pell. The pain in my shoulder distracted me. What . . .*' Shadow's voice was full of concern, but a sudden whooshing noise drew her attention away.

Out of the murky snow-filled sky emerged the unmistakeable shape of a night dragon. Shadow tensed, her muscles bunching as she prepared to get up and fight. To her surprise, rather than launching an attack, the dragon landed in silence behind the strangely organised rows of animals. Incredibly, not a single creature so much as flinched at the huge new arrival. Rather than challenging her, the dragon meekly joined the back row of animals and waited, seemingly in a sort of trance. The dragon's rider slid down to stand alongside her, similarly in thrall.

Muscles still tense, Shadow waited. A wary few moments passed, but still the night dragon made no move to attack. Confused, Shadow lifted her head on her long neck and turned to her rider. She was just in time to see Pell's hands plunge into the open saddlebag and emerge again clutching the dark orb. Shadow recoiled. The globe was pulsating with dark, repulsive energy, and there was a strange mistiness about it that had not been apparent when it had first formed on the plinth. She could see a fine forest of thin, wraithlike tendrils forming across the surface of the orb, spurting from its surface and writhing with a life of their own.

The look on Pell's face matched the horror Shadow felt in his mind. She turned her head again to look at the lines of animals standing around her in a perfect semi-circle. Hares, foxes, birds of many kinds, a solitary bear, the dragon and her rider – all stood, or sat, as silently as they had approached. In all her long years, Shadow had never seen anything like it before. It was eerie. They looked as if they had been enchanted. They were standing absolutely still. Mesmerised. Waiting for something to happen.

'NOOOOOOOOOO!'

Pell cried the single word aloud and in his mind with equal intensity. He felt the orb do it. And, through the link, Shadow felt it too. The misty tendrils suddenly shot out like darts from the surface of the orb and a pulse of energy simultaneously surged through Pell's body. Each tendril raced through the air like an arrow to attach itself to one of the waiting creatures, dragon and rider included. To Shadow's surprise, not one of them so much as flinched. Only she and Pell did not have tendrils attached to their chests.

For a moment Shadow felt Pell's horrified awareness with total clarity. He was like the anchor point of a giant spider's web, but she instinctively knew that what he was holding was far worse. There was a second surge of energy and the tendrils abruptly sucked back as one into the orb. At that same moment, each creature the tendrils had touched – the dragon, the rider, and every last animal arrayed before them – dropped soundlessly into the snow: dead.

Chapter Three
Hide and Seek

Kira sat up straight, craning her neck to scan the swirling white curtain of snow falling behind them. She could see no sign of the night dragon she knew was there. Suddenly another piercing scream ripped through the air. This time it came from ahead of them. Fang stopped beating his wings and started to glide, deliberately slowing his forward speed as he considered their options.

'*Have we flown into a trap?*' Kira asked, her heart racing.

'*The night dragons know we're here, but I don't think they can see us,*' Fang replied. '*We haven't exactly been sneaking along. I imagine they anticipated our flying this way and were lying in wait. They will have sensed us coming, much as we sensed their approach at our last encounter, but the weather has foiled their ambush.*

It appears they're trying to spook us into doing something foolish.'

'Just flying in this weather is foolish! What do they expect us to do that's more idiotic than this?'

'They are trying to panic us,' Fang explained, sounding as calm as ever. 'In this sort of weather it's easy to become disoriented and fly into the side of a mountain. They are trying to engineer a convenient accident.'

'Where are the others? Are they all right?'

There was a short pause and Kira felt Fang communicating with the other dragons, though she could not hear what was said.

'Each dragon is working alone now,' he reported. 'It's almost impossible to keep a safe formation position anyway. We have agreed to try to meet at the edge of the range some way south of here. We don't have a particular meeting place in mind. No one knows the geography around here very well, so we don't have a suitable landmark. It might take a while to find everyone again in the dark, but at least we all know roughly where the others are going.'

'So we're on our own,' Kira breathed thoughtfully, more to herself than to Fang. 'Good. At least we don't have to worry about looking out for the others.'

No sooner had the words passed her lips than she

began to feel guilty. Was it right to run away and leave the others at the mercy of the night dragons?

She leaned forwards again, streamlining herself against Fang's back. The lower she got, the more the wind seemed to lose its icy bite. The easiest option was to run, but was the easy way the best way? Being a dusk dragon, Fang could use his chameleon-like ability to blend into any background. His camouflage made him impossible to see in the falling snow. The night dragons would never catch him. The same could not be said for the others, though. Firestorm's blue scales, Shadow's black scales and particularly Aurora's bright golden scales would make each of them visible from some distance.

Kira sighed as she realised her conscience would not allow her to think only of herself. She had not wanted to become a part of the dragonrider community, but she was now involved in an important quest that required the four dragons and their riders to work together towards a common goal. Like it or not, they were a team.

There was an alternative to running. She could turn the situation into a hunt – swap roles from hunted to hunter. It was what she did best. If she and Fang began hunting down the night dragons, her friends would have more of a chance to escape.

'What do you think, Fang?' she asked, aware of his

presence in her mind. She could feel him listening to her thoughts as she played through the mental debate. '*Should we make a run for it, or stick around and cause some trouble?*'

'*That depends on what you want to achieve,*' he replied. '*I can see value in trying to confuse the night dragons, but I'm not strong enough to fight them. The night dragons are all far larger than the biggest dusk dragon. Any one of them would be more than a match for me in a straight fight.*'

'*I try never to get into a fight with my prey,*' Kira assured him. '*Confusing the night dragons would be great. It will give our friends a chance to escape unseen. We should be able to slip past the night dragons at any time in these conditions.*'

'*True, providing I don't lose track of my bearings,*' he pointed out. '*I don't want to find myself inadvertently flying back the way we just came. We might deceive this party only to run into Segun and his men by accident.*'

'*No. That wouldn't be good,*' Kira agreed.

'*Also, this party knows there is a dusk dragon in our group, so they will be alert to my abilities. It will not be easy to fool them. Are you sure you want to do this? It could be a lot more dangerous than you think.*'

'*No, I'm not sure,*' Kira admitted. '*But I can't just let the others be hunted down. We have to do something.*'

'Very well. Hold on tight. I have an idea that might work.'

Kira wanted to discuss his idea, but she was given no chance. She felt Fang reach out with his mind. A moment later he turned to the left and drew in a deep breath. The bellow took her completely by surprise. She had never heard Fang roar like that before. Even his challenging roar during the attack by the dragonhunters had sounded nothing like this. On and on it went, seeming all the longer because she knew it had the full attention of any night dragon for miles around. What did he think he was doing? If she had known what he was about to do, she would have thought twice about playing the heroine.

The tone of Fang's bellow carried a challenge that said, 'Come and get me if you think you're strong enough'. No self-respecting night dragon would be able to turn down such a taunt. Kira huddled down tight to Fang's back. Her eyes scanned the sky around them for signs of the night dragons she knew would be homing in.

It did not take long for the first dragon shape to loom out of the murky snow. It came from ahead. Fang camouflaged instantly, disappearing from under Kira. His unnerving ability to blend into his surroundings did not normally worry her, but this time Fang simultaneously folded his wings and dropped abruptly to dip under the incoming night dragon. Her stomach lurched towards her throat. It was a particularly horrible sensation, because it felt as if Fang had really vanished into thin air and left her to fall. The feeling was short-lived. Fang snapped his wings out, soaring underneath the night dragon and climbing back to his level.

No sooner had Fang reached the night dragon's level than he reappeared and roared again. His reward was a screech of frustration from the dragon he had just avoided and then a second one that sounded more surprised. Then there was silence. Both screeches appeared to have come from the same direction and distance.

'*They nearly collided,*' Fang said, sounding smug. His voice echoed strangely inside her head, but Kira was quick to recognise the phenomenon. He had narrowed their mental link to prevent other dragons from tapping into their thoughts. '*It has shaken them up. I can feel their relief. They know they were lucky. Hold on tight. It's time to lead them on a bit of a dance.*'

Kira did not reply. She concentrated on holding on as tightly as she could to the pommel of the saddle. When she had suggested causing trouble, she had imagined directing Fang in a stealthy hunt and distracting the night dragons with hit-and-run attacks. This open taunting was not her style and she felt very uncomfortable with her dragon's tactics. The cold did not help. Her mind felt slow and fogged, and she was fast losing sensation in her extremities. Although she would have been perfectly at home playing hide-and-seek with any of the deadly animals in the warm savannah of Racafi, this three-dimensional game in the freezing, snow-filled air of the mountains of northern Isaa made her feel terribly small and lost.

'*Turning left,*' Fang warned. He roared again, disappearing from under her a second time and suddenly dipping his left wing into a hard turn. Once again the great night dragons converged on the spot from which he had issued his challenge. Despite his warning, Kira was surprised by the abruptness of the turn. Clinging on with all her strength, she held fast to the saddle, but by the time they rolled back to wings level, her arms were shaking with the effort.

Fang reappeared under her. He roared again. This time three night dragon voices responded with screeches filled with anger and frustration.

'*You've certainly got their attention, Fang,*' Kira observed, trying to stay calm. '*Are they all after us now?*'

'Yes. All three are nearby. They have all answered my challenge.'

'Great!' she said, feeling about as far from great as possible. 'Now what do we do?'

'We fly rings around them, of course,' Fang replied, sounding surprised by the question. 'Keep them busy long enough for the others to get away and then sneak off ourselves.'

He turned back towards the night dragons, powering upwards this time and disappearing again. Kira could feel him searching the area ahead and below them with his eyes and his mind. She shivered. What if they anticipated his move? Suddenly three dark dragon-shaped outlines appeared in close formation ahead and slightly below them. They loomed unnaturally large against the backdrop of falling white flecks. Fang materialised again and dived at the huge shapes. With the advantage of height and surprise, Fang's appearance caused them to scatter as he swooped down at them like a striking falcon only to disappear again at the last second. On silent wings he soared back up into the relative safety of the murky cloud.

Again and again Fang taunted the night dragons, each time manoeuvring to confuse or disorient them. With every flashing encounter his three adversaries became wiser to his tactics. Gradually they started to coordinate their efforts against him. Kira could do nothing other than hang on. It was not a pleasant sensation to have to place all her trust in Fang even though he was her partner for life. She was very much used to controlling her own destiny, but there was nothing she could do to help. Flying tactics were Fang's domain. He was old and wily. She knew better than to interfere, but as the night dragons became more organised, so the game they were playing became progressively more dangerous.

'*I think that's enough, Fang,*' she said eventually. '*We've pushed our luck to the limit. Let's get out of here.*'

'*I agree,*' he replied. '*I was not expecting the pincer response they pulled on the last run. They're no fools. I can't feel any of our friends nearby, so we've achieved our aim.*'

Fang stayed camouflaged as he dipped his right wing and entered a descending spiral. He kept the turn tight, but not horribly so. Kira looked down in an effort to see the ground. When Fang levelled his wings and began to beat them again in the familiar rhythm he used for distance flying, Kira was surprised to realise that she had been looking without seeing for some time. She had become so used to the milky whiteness inside the murky snowstorm that she had not detected the subtly different white of the carpet covering the valley floor below.

A burning sensation rushed up from her stomach to the back of her throat and a sour taste settled on her tongue. She did not know if Fang had seen the ground approaching, or if he had an inbuilt sense of how high he was. Either way, the shock of comprehension when she registered how low they had come made her appreciate her dragon's abilities all the more. Fang could have crashed into the ground and she would never have seen it coming. It was a scary thought.

They flew along the valley basin in total silence. The snow continued to fall around them, but the visibility was sufficient for Fang to navigate safely.

'Do you think the night dragons are following us?' she asked, as they turned left into a narrower valley.

'It's hard to say,' Fang replied. 'They were still adapting tactics to try to catch me in the act of taunting them when we left. They will think our disappearance is another ruse to begin with, but I doubt they will take long to realise the truth.'

The light was fading fast. The dark clouds overhead made it feel more like dusk than late afternoon. Kira quickly lost all sense of which way they were heading. All the valleys looked similar.

Some were wider than others, but all were buried in snow. Through her mental link with Fang she felt his confidence that they were heading in the right direction, but she had no way of helping or checking.

When the valley walls finally disappeared, Kira heaved a sigh of relief. Snow was still falling, but the sky was definitely lighter. Without the menace of huge peaks looming to either side of them, Kira instinctively began to relax, and the cold suddenly began to feel more intense than ever.

Fang turned to the right, seeking to parallel the mountain range southwards. Assuming they had safely navigated clear of the peaks, her companions would be doing the same. Kira could feel herself succumbing to the cold. Having felt its insidious bite before, she was now aware of the danger. The signs were unmistakeable.

'*I'm sorry, Fang, but if we don't land soon I'm going to freeze,*' she warned.

'*I know,*' he replied. '*I've been looking for somewhere safe to set down for a while now, but I've not sensed anywhere useable. I'm not sure what to do.*'

'*I think we're just going to have to land and make the best of what's around,*' she said, her body trembling violently. '*Can you see any woodland? I know it's dangerous, but I'm going to need a fire to warm me up.*'

Kira held her breath as she sensed Fang straining to see through snow and mist.

'Yes,' he said. '*There is woodland not far to our left, but . . .*'

'But what?' she gasped aloud. 'What's wrong?'

'*It's probably nothing,*' he said slowly, but he sounded troubled. '*For a moment I felt a flicker of something – a presence.*'

'*Another dragon?*' she asked.

Fang did not answer straight away. She could feel him straining as he swept the area ahead with his mind. Kira could just make out the trees of a pine forest. The treetops were laden with snow, but the conical shapes and the freckles of dark green amongst the shroud of white were unmistakeable.

'*I don't think so,*' he replied. '*It was such a fleeting impression that it's impossible to be certain. Whatever it was, it's not there now. The snow must be confusing my senses. We'll land.*'

Chapter Four

Into the Night

Pell was stunned. The after-image of the moment of mass death was etched in his mind. He stood transfixed as he stared at the rows of lifeless bodies in the snow. What had just happened? The dark orb throbbed relentlessly in his hands. He felt sick. It had used him. It was still using him. He could feel its power coursing through his body. Tears formed in his eyes. He had no control. All he could do was stand and look at the aftermath of the orb's destructive power.

Suddenly the pressure was gone. He staggered backwards, reeling in a dizzy circle. Pain spiked through his head as if a huge needle had been driven through his forehead and deep into his skull. Released from the compulsion to hold it, he pushed the black globe away from his body. It flew through the air and landed in soft snow a few feet away, unharmed.

One hand went instinctively to his forehead to massage the spot from where the pain seemed to originate. For the briefest instant, Pell felt an overwhelming desire to rush over and smash the orb into a million tiny pieces – an eye for an eye, a life for a life. Was the orb alive? he wondered. It certainly seemed to have an awareness of its surroundings. How else could it have controlled him and selectively ignored both him and Shadow with its tendrils? He was not sure he wanted an answer to that question.

'Pell?' Shadow's voice sounded lost and uncertain in his mind, but he sensed that she shared his pain.

He ignored her, stumbling forwards a few paces before finding his balance. Control restored, he placed his feet with care, stepping between the dead animals until he reached the dragonrider. The man was lying face down in the snow about two paces from his unmoving dragon. Pell's throat felt tight as he crouched by the body and tentatively reached under the man's torso to roll him over. He was heavy, but Pell was determined.

The man's expression was exactly as it had been in the instant of his death. His features were slack and his eyes wide open and unseeing, just as they had been during his final few moments. Pell's stomach churned as he closed the man's eyelids with trembling fingers.

'Pell?'

'I killed him,' he croaked, tears forming in his eyes. 'I killed them all.'

'*It wasn't you, Pell,*' Shadow soothed, her voice stroking his mind with a velvet touch. '*It was the orb. You did not call them here. You cannot blame yourself for this.*'

'Can't I?' he spat, turning to face her. His eyes were burning with a fierce fanaticism. 'Can't I? My hands held the orb, Shadow. My hands! This man, this dragon, all these animals – gone, because I wasn't strong enough to control my hands.'

Shadow was silent for a moment. She had never seen her rider so distraught. Nothing in all her many years of travelling the world had prepared her for this.

'*Fang told me the first orb gave off an aura of blood,*' she said thoughtfully. '*He said the orb's aura drew predators from miles around and drove them into a frenzy of bloodlust. It seems this orb also has an aura. This orb also attracts, but it then feeds on the life force of those it draws. It doesn't seem to do it constantly like the day orb, or we would have had visitors before*' now. The orbs are powerful, Pell. I doubt any human could resist the will of an orb.'

Shadow lifted her head high and looked around. The light was fading fast.

'*Sundown!*' she said suddenly.

'What?'

'*Sundown. The orb killed exactly at sundown,*' she explained.

'How do you know that?' Pell asked, looking first around at the darkening sky and then back at his dragon.

'*Just as a dawn dragon has an affinity with dawn, so we night dragons can tell when night is about to begin. Let me know if you start to feel the urge to take out the orb again, but I have a feeling it will not happen until the same time tomorrow. That gives us a day to work out how to prevent it from killing more innocents. We need to find the others. Maybe one of them will be able to help. One thing is certain – the sooner we can get the orb to the Oracle, the better.*'

'I won't argue with that,' Pell said, a shudder rippling down his spine. 'But are you sure we should look for the others? What if it kills them as well? I had no control, Shadow. It was horrible. I don't know if I can cope with carrying it any more.'

'*You have to, Pell. This is our duty. We have to get the orb to the Oracle in Orupee. The others share this*

43

responsibility. Don't worry. We'll warn them – make sure they're ready to run if it starts happening again. Try to be careful. Don't touch it directly. Wrap it in your spare clothing and pack it at the bottom of the saddle-bag. Make it as difficult to reach as possible. That might give us the extra moments we need.'

Pell did not like to point out that wrapping it deep in his saddlebag was exactly what he had done the first time. He did not want to go anywhere near the gruesome globe, but he knew he had no choice. Shadow was right. The quest was all that remained. They had both suffered a great deal to win the orb. He had come too far to give up now.

Picking his way back through the rows of bodies, Pell returned to the base of the rock where his open saddlebag sat in the snow. Shadow moved out of his way, uncoiling from the great boulder and shaking the snow from her back and wings. Pell reached inside the bag and drew out his spare cloak. He turned and looked down at the black ball in the snow. It appeared inert and harmless, like a mammoth black pearl deliberately set into a hollow of purest white.

If it had not been for the horrors of the last few minutes, Pell would have scorned anyone else for being reluctant to pick it up. Every muscle in his body was taut as he spread his cloak over the orb. Even with it covered, he could feel his heart hammering against his ribs. He reached down to collect it and paused. With a flash of insight he realised that this was how Nolita felt every time she approached her dragon.

The thought that he was acting like the cringeing girl hardened his resolve. He grabbed the orb and quickly wrapped it over and over in the cloth before stuffing it down into the base of his saddle-bag. Shuffling everything else around in the leather bag, he buried the bundle under as many things as he could. His fingers trembled as he fumbled with the buckles.

'Well done, Pell,' Shadow said smoothly. 'Let's go. The griffins will have released Segun and his men from the valley by now.'

The conditions were little better than they had been when they landed. The wind was still whipping the snow through the air and visibility was very limited, but Pell could feel that Shadow was stronger after her rest. He could feel her confidence through the bond. No sooner had they launched into the darkening sky than she began to use her ability to silence the sound of her wing-beats.

Pell felt safe sitting on Shadow's back inside the unnaturally silent bubble. The light faded fast and the wind tugged at his clothing with cold fingers, but the silence had a strange way of taking the sting out of the wind's bitter chill. He also perceived something of the strange echo navigation sense Shadow used when flying at night. Even though her vision was limited, he was confident she would not crash into anything. Much like a bat, she was perfectly at home flying blind in the dark.

It was hard to keep track of the passage of time. Shadow did not want to risk following the others directly, as this was likely to put them in the path of their pursuers again. Instead she stayed amongst the mountains, threading through valley after valley in a zigzagging route southwards before finally turning left and heading for the edge of the mountain range. Once they were clear, they turned south, paralleling the line of peaks and flying on into the night.

'*I've located Elian and Aurora,*' Shadow announced suddenly.

Pell was relieved. He was freezing cold and desperately tired. He wanted to find shelter, have a hot drink, eat some food and catch a few hours of sleep. If Elian had stopped, then so could he.

'*Where?*' he asked.

'*Not far,*' Shadow replied, her voice encouraging. '*They are holed up in a small wood just ahead and to our left. Hang on tight. We're going down.*'

'Great. How did you find them?'

'I didn't. Aurora sensed me coming. She has given me directions. We should be there in less than a minute.'

Pell was so relieved it hurt inside.

'Are the girls there as well?' he asked.

There was a pause and Pell could feel Shadow reaching ahead with her mind.

'I don't think so,' she said eventually. 'If they are there, Fire and Fang are hiding their minds from me most effectively. I can feel no trace of them.'

Pell decided it would be a relief if they were not there. Kira brought out the worst in him. Everything she said seemed to spark him to anger. And Nolita was no less annoying. Her cringing fear and maddening little rituals drove him to distraction. All that hand-washing! It beggared belief that she was a dragonrider at all.

They descended steeply, adjusting their course to the left and dropping down into the darkness. Pell could not see a thing. He felt, more than saw, the ground approach. An instant before Shadow adjusted the angle of her wings to arrest their rate of descent, his buttocks clenched instinctively and his stomach muscles tightened in anticipation. Shadow back-winged to a gentle landing. Falling snow brushed at Pell's face with tickling gentleness as it fell in a thick swarm around him.

'Where are they, Shadow?' he asked aloud. 'I can't see a thing.'

'In the trees just ahead,' she replied. 'No more than about fifty of your paces, I'd say.'

'I can't even see the trees,' he grunted. 'Shall I get down, or can you get to them with me on your back?'

'I suggest you get down,' Shadow said. 'The pines are quite thick. I will have to squeeze between the trees to reach them.'

Pell knew from past experience that trying to get in amongst densely packed trees on a dragon's back could be uncomfortable. In this light he would not be able to see the branches coming. At least if he was on foot he could feel his way through the needle-laden boughs.

Stiff with cold, he slid down Shadow's left flank and landed with a thump into the ankle-deep snow. The shock of landing transmitted through his legs and up his back, carrying a ripple of pain that highlighted just how cold-soaked he was. He grimaced as he straightened up, rubbing briefly at his thighs and lower back before taking his first careful steps forwards.

The fifty paces felt more like five hundred. He had to feel his way into the darkness, taking each blind step carefully for fear of a branch in the eye, or of stepping into an unseen hole. The dim light from Elian's hidden fire was not visible until Pell was little more than ten paces away from where Elian was sitting. He had cleverly built it on the far side of a fallen tree, in the crook between the trunk and one of the larger branches. It was tucked almost underneath, which restricted the light, but ensured that the heat would all reflect outwards in a specific direction.

All Pell could see of Elian was his head and shoulders over the fallen tree trunk that blocked his path, but he could tell that the younger boy was scanning the darkness, looking for him.

'Evening, Elian,' Pell said, trying to sound casual. 'Nice spot you've found here.' In his own ears his voice sounded hard and clumsy as his cold lips struggled to shape the sounds.

'Pell! Come on over. I've been waiting for you,' Elian replied, sounding relieved to hear Pell's voice. 'Have you seen the girls?'

'No, I was going to ask you the same. Did the other night dragons follow you?'

'If they did, they didn't catch up with us,' Elian said, watching Pell climb awkwardly over the fallen tree. 'Ra told me Fang deliberately stayed to draw them into a chase and keep them off our backs. How about you?'

Pell hunched down next to Elian and stared into the tiny flickering flames. He held his hands out, warming them as the pause grew into an uncomfortable silence. A series of loud cracking noises announced the arrival of Shadow, pushing through the pines and snapping the branches she couldn't squeeze past. Pell could see her red eyes glowing in the darkness. He felt comforted by her presence, but was still unsure how to answer Elian's question. It was hard to know where to start. Feelings of guilt and remorse returned in force, churning deep in the pit of his stomach.

'We met one of the night dragons,' he said eventually.

'What happened?' Elian prompted, his tone cautious after the awkward silence that had followed his previous question.

'Dragon and rider are both dead.'

'Oh,' Elian said softly. He fell silent, leaving the obvious question unasked.

Pell turned to look at the boy from Racafi, but Elian did not meet his eyes. Did the boy really think that he and Shadow had deliberately killed a fellow dragon and rider? It appeared that way. Indignant, Pell blurted out the truth.

'The orb killed them.'

The words hung in the air.

'The orb?' Elian asked, his voice rising with surprise and his eyes finally turning to meet Pell's steady gaze. 'How?'

Pell told him. In halting snatches, he described the pull of the orb and the strange arrival of the small host of animals. To begin with the words came slowly, but the more he spoke the faster the words came, until they tumbled from his mouth like a waterfall. Vivid memories flashed through his mind's eye as he relived the horror of the orb's power. Elian sat in silence, his jaw slowly dropping as Pell reached the terrible climax of his story.

'Gods alive!' he breathed as Pell fell silent. 'And I thought the first orb was dangerous! We need to get that thing to the Oracle's cave – and fast!'

'I agree, except for one thing,' Pell said.

'What's that?'

'There can't be any *we* this time. I'm going to have to do this alone.'

Chapter Five
White Terror

Kira had always been proud of her woodcraft skills, but in Racafi she had never had to deal with cold like this. Her hands felt worse than useless. They were clumsy lumps of flesh on the ends of her arms. Her fingers felt weak and stiff and she had lost all dexterity. Muscles throughout her body ached with the fatigue of deep cold. Tears of frustration began to well in her eyes. She blinked rapidly to prevent them escaping.

'Damn, damn, damn!' she cursed as she threw her flint and steel down in frustration.

It was almost dark. The snow was still falling heavily and the temperature was dropping fast. For all her skills and knowledge of survival learned in the Racafian savannah, she could not get a fire to light. She knew that to stop trying now was to invite the cold embrace of death. Tired though she was, and angry at her inadequacies, Kira could not give up. Quitting was not in her nature.

'Why can't you breathe fire like Firestorm?' she muttered at Fang, glaring at her dragon with accusing eyes. 'I bet Nolita isn't cold. Even if she hasn't got wood to burn, he can always heat the rock for her.'

Her dragon did not respond with words, but she felt his love and concern flood through their special bond. The sensation triggered instant feelings of guilt.

Fang had hatched from his egg in the twilight time after the sun had set, but before true night had fallen. As a result he had grown into a dusk dragon and developed the unique camouflage abilities of those rare dragons born between sundown and darkness. He could no more become a day dragon than he could change the colour of the sky.

'Sorry, Fang,' she added through gritted teeth. 'That was uncalled for. I didn't mean it. I just . . .'

She could not finish the sentence. Her brain felt as frozen as her limbs. With a groan she bent down and recovered her fire-starting materials and resumed her efforts, striking showers of sparks again and again across the tinder and kindling. Every time she sprayed the stars of light across the tiny pile of sticks, dark shadows leapt, teasing the corners of her vision. Tall trees loomed over her, crowding together like giants poised to stomp and crush. With increasing frequency she found herself looking around for signs of danger, but there was nothing to see. The black pillars of the tree trunks stood solid and motionless.

'What's the matter, Kira?' she asked herself aloud through chattering teeth. 'You've been alone in the woods lots of times. Besides, you're not alone. You've got a dragon to protect you from . . .'

What? What was it that she felt she needed protection from? If the night dragons came close, Fang could conceal them both with ease. No normal predator with any sense would come near them, so what was it that had her so on edge? The atmosphere felt heavy with black menace. All was silent. But there were no burning eyes watching her out of the darkness. She could not see or hear anything moving.

'I'm getting paranoid,' she muttered.

'*No, you're not,*' Fang said. '*I sense it too, but I don't know what it is that I'm feeling. I thought I felt something before we landed. There is something bad about this place. I think we should go.*'

'*I'm too cold, Fang,*' she told him stubbornly. '*I need to warm up before we go anywhere. I don't think*

I'll be able to stay on your back unless I get some blood circulating through my hands and feet.'

'Well, whatever you're going to do, make it quick.'

Suddenly it all became clear to Kira. The nervousness she was feeling was not her own. It was Fang's. Her dragon was transmitting his discomfort into her mind through the bond. The thought that this huge powerful creature might be afraid of a spooky old forest made her snigger. She could not help herself. It built inside her, bubbling up with irresistible momentum and before she knew it, she was giggling like a little girl.

Fang turned his head and fixed her with a hard stare.

'There is nothing funny about this place, Kira,' he said firmly.

'Yes there is,' she countered. 'What's funny is you! I never realised dragons could be afraid of the dark.'

'I'm not.'

'Then what are you afraid of?' she challenged. 'I can feel your fear, Fang. I thought it was me getting the jitters. Now I know it's you. It's like Nolita and Firestorm, only in reverse.'

The sound was barely more than a whisper, but with mind-boggling swiftness, Fang struck. His jaws snapped open, revealing his vicious rows of inward-curving teeth. The prominent longer fang for which he was named flashed towards her so fast that she barely had time to register what was happening. Her reaction was to suck in a sharp breath with which to scream, but before she had a chance to utter a sound, Fang's head whipped straight past her and he bit down into the snow.

As he lifted his head again, Kira saw something pale and long, wriggling and writhing in his jaws.

'What the hell's that?' she gasped as she began to make out details.

The creature was long and segmented like a worm, but it was as thick as her arm. She could see no eyes, but even in the deepening darkness beneath the trees Kira could make out the mouth full of jagged, icicle-like teeth. Whatever it was, the creature was hideous.

'*Ice worm!*' Fang said, his voice in her mind now alive with fear. '*Get on my back. Now! You must get out of the snow. Come on!*'

Initially, Kira could not move. Fang's panic rooted her to the spot. The crunch as the dragon's teeth sheered through the ice worm's plated exterior was horrible. He flicked his head, casting the remains of the worm as far as he could. Where the creature's body landed, the snow instantly exploded in a frenzy of thrashing, writhing serpentine bodies. The speed with which they moved was electrifying. All the hair at the back of Kira's neck stood on end.

Fang pounced. There was no other description for his movement. It was catlike. One moment he was in one place, the next he was leaping forwards. As he landed, the snow to either side of his front feet erupted as pinned ice worms fought to free themselves from under his weight. That they had not been instantly crushed did not go unnoticed by Kira. These creatures were incredibly tough.

'It's a swarm! Get out of the snow, Kira! Get out of the snow! They're deadly!' Fang cried in her mind, his voice carrying a desperate edge. 'I can't stop them. There are too many.'

This time his words got through. Kira's brain, slowed as it was by the cold, processed Fang's fear, the speed of the creatures, the danger of the situation and finally forced her cold-soaked body into action. She stumbled the few short paces through the snow and tried to scramble up Fang's foreleg to the relative safety of his back, still clutching her flint and steel.

As Kira lifted her trailing leg out of the snow, pain tore through her right calf and she screamed in agony. An ice worm had bitten deep into the flesh and was now dangling behind her as she tried in vain to drag herself higher from the white surface. She could feel its teeth sinking deeper and deeper into her muscle, slicing through her flesh and sending a wave of icy coldness up and down her leg.

Fang's head twisted on his long neck and with a touch of finesse she would not have believed possible of her dragon, he twitched the tail of the great worm out so he could catch its body between his teeth. There was another sickening crunch as he sheared the worm in two, but to Kira's horror, the head end of the creature did not let go of her leg. It thrashed around, tearing her flesh even more, its teeth clamping tighter and tighter.

Screaming with every scrap of energy her lungs could find, she reached down with her right hand and began hitting it with the flint. The surface of the worm was slippery like ice and hard as steel. Her efforts proved worse than useless. Rather than let go, the worm tried all the harder to bite right through to the bone.

'Heat!' Fang told her, his voice frantic. '*Use the flint and steel. Ice worms cannot stand fire.*'

Kira twisted so that she could sit on Fang's shoulder. Below her the snow was heaving in waves as a multitude of worms attacked from all sides. Despite dozens latching onto the dragon's body, he remained motionless for fear of tipping Kira from her precarious perch. Reaching down with both hands this time, she scraped the steel against the flint and sent a shower of bright golden sparks across the worm's body.

The dying creature's response was instant. It could not let go fast enough. It released its grip and fell away from her, sliding down Fang's foreleg only to be consumed in seconds by the thrashing mass of ice worms below.

'*Well done. Now get into the saddle, Kira,*' Fang urged. '*I need to move. My scales are tough, but this looks like a big swarm. Even a dragon cannot hope to survive long against a sustained attack by ice worms.*'

She turned, wincing as lines of pain shot up her injured leg. It only took her a few seconds, but it quickly became apparent that even this short time might prove fatal. Hundreds of worms had gained purchase on Fang's body. Having gained a hold with their teeth, the worms had then burrowed back, tail first into the frozen ground and were now holding Fang in place like a web of living ropes. She could feel his muscles bunching and straining as he tried to lift his belly from the ground, but he could no longer move.

The pain in her leg was forgotten. Her fear was absolute. Worse – she could feel it shared and amplified by her dragon. The snowy carpet under the trees was alive with rippling movement as more and more worms swam through the snow towards them. They were trapped and she could see no way out. Without a miracle, she and Fang were going to die a horrible death.

It was strange. Normally flying hazards served to increase Nolita's fears, but the onset of the snowstorm had actually helped her to control her emotions. The dancing white flakes provided a mesmerising show that held her attention and deadened her mind to reality. Perhaps it was because it reminded her of midwinter feasts back home in Cemaria – happy times with family and friends. Perhaps it was the subtle way it played with her vision, never allowing her focus to settle at any one distance. Whatever the reason, Nolita was surprisingly content to be flying on Firestorm's back this afternoon.

It was cold, of course. Bitterly cold. But the rhythm of Firestorm's wingbeats and the gentle rising and falling motion of his body had become so familiar over the past two weeks that her fear of falling from his back had dimmed. It was the first physical contact with her dragon each time she flew that she dreaded the most. The act of reaching up and touching her dragon's leg in order to mount him still filled her mind with black dread.

She knew it was irrational. Through her bond with Firestorm, she could feel his thoughts and emotions. To begin with she had been convinced he was trying to deceive her, but she could no longer deny the truth. The dragon cared deeply for her. But even her intimate knowledge of his feelings did not curb her physical reaction to his size and appearance. Nolita had learned ways to counter her fear of heights whilst flying, but she had found nothing that could help dim her reaction to Firestorm's size and initial proximity.

A night dragon's screaming cry rent the air behind her. The sound struck her with a force that was almost physical. She had allowed the snow to lull her vision and detach her mind from her situation. An attack by night dragons had always been a possibility, but she had not expected it to come so soon. Where were her friends? Elian was to her left, riding Aurora, but he was barely visible and there was no sign of the others. In the blink of an eye her fears were back with full force.

'Hang on,' Fire's voice warned in her mind. 'It's too dangerous to stay with the others. We're going it alone.'

Nolita did not reply. Instead, she clung with all her might to the pommel of her saddle. Firestorm dipped his right wing, turning positively away from Aurora for a few seconds before turning back to parallel his original course.

Another scream sounded. This one seemed to come from directly ahead. There was a short pause and then a bellowing roar unlike anything Nolita had ever heard before. Her heart was pounding hard and fast. A huge shadow suddenly blossomed ahead and slightly above them. It was a night dragon. There was no mistaking the sheer size of it. It cut across them, angling towards the source of the huge roar that had reverberated a few seconds before.

'It's all right. The roar was Fang,' Firestorm informed her. 'He's going to draw the night dragons off and give the rest of us a chance to get away. It's lucky he got their attention, or that one would have seen us for sure.'

Nolita wanted to feel relief, but she was too scared. The dancing white curtain of snow that had lulled her mind moments earlier had suddenly become a white veil of terror. Behind it lurked unknown horrors waiting to pounce.

'Calm your breathing, Nolita,' Firestorm continued, his voice soothing and gentle in her mind. 'You're breathing too fast. If you continue, you will overload your body and pass out. That would not be *good. Breathe slowly. Think calm thoughts. Tranquil. Concentrate on each breath. Yes. That's it. Slower. Not so deep. Well done.'*

Little by little, Nolita regained control. The irony that a dragon, the primary source of her fear, should also prove its antidote was not lost on her. Still tense with fear, but back in command of her body, Nolita concentrated on staying in the saddle.

Another roar sounded behind them. It sounded like Fang again.

Kira's so brave, she thought. If only I could be more like her. The cold wind numbed the skin on her face and at her extremities. 'If only I could find something that would numb fear the same way,' she added aloud in a whisper that was lost on the wind. 'If only . . .'

Chapter Six
A Night in the Woods

'Haven't you learned anything on this quest, Pell?' Elian sighed. He looked across the fire at the older boy and shook his head sadly. 'You can't work alone. None of us can. This quest is something we're supposed to do together. The Oracle chose us to work as a team. Look what happened last time you tried.'

Pell stared back, his body tense and his face defiant. 'But the orb could kill you at the next sunset,' he protested. 'I don't want your death on my conscience as well.'

'So you're going to play the selfish card again,' Elian responded, his tone mocking. 'I want this. I don't want that. Listen to yourself! You think you're being all heroic and selfless, but you're not thinking straight. If you and Shadow try to do this alone, the orb will kill many innocent creatures and possibly more people and dragons. Using Ra's abilities we could possibly get to the Oracle without ever seeing another sunset.'

'Right!' Pell drawled. 'I suppose you and Aurora are going to stop the sun in its tracks for me while I deliver the orb. Excellent! I'm almost tempted to take you along with me just to see you try.'

Elian sighed again. Pell was enough to drive even the most patient of people to distraction. It was a shame, he reflected. There were many things about him that Elian found enviable: the boy's physical strength, striking good looks, fitness and determination. Unfortunately, his manner and appalling lack of sensitivity made him easy to dislike.

'That's just the point, Pell. We can stop the sun,' he said. 'Don't you remember how we got to the night dragon enclave?'

'Ah, yes! Of course!' Pell said, his voice rising as if he had just made a momentous discovery. 'The other world – the flying machines and magical weapons. An entertaining fantasy to pass the time, I'm sure. Unfortunately, I have to deal with reality, Elian. The orb is deadly. I don't have the luxury of daydreams.'

Elian stared at him and took several calming breaths to keep from losing his temper. It was incredible! All this time Pell had not believed a word about their adventure. They had travelled through gateways that only dawn dragons could create – gateways that had carried them into the strange land of France, where many hundreds of thousands of men were engaged in a terrible war. They had risked their lives in a strange world to rescue him, but he refused to believe it. It seemed likely Pell did not believe Nolita had gained her orb either. Given the unusual skills each of their dragons possessed, Elian had assumed Pell's acceptance of Aurora's ability to open the gateways between worlds. Now it appeared he would need to see first hand to believe it.

'The night won't last long, Pell,' Elian said, his tone as cold as the air around him. He had to work very hard to keep the rest of his response civil. 'As soon as the others get here and the sun rises, you'll see. I'm going to get some sleep. I suggest you do the same while we have the chance.'

Pell did not reply. Neither did he move. Elian gritted his teeth at the boy's stubbornness and eased down onto his side, drawing his blankets around him.

'What if the others don't find us, Elian?' Aurora asked. *'I've not heard anything of Fire and Fang since we split up. If we go through to the other world, they will*

have to escape the night dragons on their own. I don't want to abandon them.'

'Let's hope it doesn't come to that,' Elian replied, snuggling down as best he could on his groundsheet next to the fire. 'That's not a choice I want to make. Can you keep watch tonight, or are you too tired?'

'Do not fear, Elian,' she replied. 'I will keep watch. Dragons can go several days without rest, if necessary.'

'Good. Let me know if you sense anything. I really need to rest while I can.'

Wrapping himself in all the blankets he had, Elian settled as close to the fire as he dared and closed his eyes. He tried to relax, but although he felt bone-weary he quickly realised that sleep would not come easily. The cold was a part of it, but by no means the main reason. Thoughts were running around inside his head like swarming flies, uncountable and confusing. Trying to follow any one through to a conclusion was impossible. Others continually intruded, dragging his mind first in one direction and then another.

This quest had seemed straightforward to begin with: find and retrieve four orbs. Framed like that it sounded as if it should be easy, so why was it difficult? Many complications arose as a result of the people the Oracle had chosen. Nolita revealed her fears even before the quest began. Pell's arrogance

67

and ego made it worse. Kira was clever and strong, but her continual clashes with Pell did not help. Then there were the complications of travelling through the other world and invoking the wrath of the leader of the night dragons. Somehow, despite these obstacles, they had secured two of the four orbs. But even the orbs possessed nasty characteristics that served to complicate matters further.

Elian mulled over the events of the past two weeks and tried to make sense of them. The more he thought about it, the harder it was to see any sense in what the Oracle had asked them to do. The dragon spirit clearly knew the nature of the orbs and had sent the plinths to their current resting places at some time in the distant past, but why? There seemed no logic in it. The plinths apparently generated the glass-like skin of the orbs, so why not just keep them in the Oracle's cave? Dragons were noble to the point of stupidity at times. He felt sure that the Oracle only needed to ask and dragons would line up to donate blood, or even the beating heart from their chests to see the Oracle reborn. So what was this quest really about?

Asking Aurora was pointless. The dragon had only one answer: this was their destiny. She saw the quest as her life purpose and did not question the reason for it. For all that she was a creature of experience, wisdom and knowledge, he felt she was blinkered by tradition.

After a while Elian heard Pell laying out his groundsheet and settling down nearby. To his annoyance, the older boy's breathing soon slowed into the slow steady rhythm of sleep. Elian felt a stab of envy. How did Pell do it? With all that he had gone through today: the trials against the night dragon rider, Dirk, Shadow's injury and then the trauma of the orb's killing spree, somehow he was still able to relax into sleep. Maybe it was exhaustion, but if that was the case, then Elian felt he should be able to do the same.

The little fire popped and snapped occasionally as it gradually ate through the small supply of sticks and melted down into a pile of glowing embers. The fallen tree reflected the heat of the tiny flames, but there was not much energy from it. Elian began to shiver and the muscles in his back and shoulders ached with tension. He tried to relax, but his efforts triggered an even more intense bout of shivering. His jaw began to ache and he suddenly realised that he had been unconsciously clenching his teeth.

'How long until dawn, Ra?' he asked eventually.

'About three hours.'

Elian groaned and sat up. He carefully added a small pile of sticks onto the remains of the fire and blew gently across the embers until they flared back into life. If I can't sleep, I might as well be warm, he thought.

The short hours of darkness dragged. The snow persisted, and the treetops creaked and swayed in the breeze. An occasional shower of icy snowflakes dropped through the thick canopy of snow-laden needles, shaken loose by the wind. The air was motionless in the lee of the fallen tree, but Elian listened intently to the voice of the breeze in the upper branches, all the time hoping to hear Firestorm and Longfang approach.

As the first hints of dawn began to lighten the eastern horizon the temperature dropped still further and Elian's heart sank with it. Where were the girls? Had the night dragons captured them? Was Segun holding them prisoner? Should he and Pell leave and concentrate on getting the dark orb to the Oracle, or should they try to find the girls first?

'*What should we do, Ra?*' he asked. He could feel his dragon listening in on his thoughts, but she had been strangely silent. Aurora normally had strong opinions, but she had not volunteered any thoughts at all during the night.

'*We should prepare to leave and hope the others arrive in time to make the decision easy,*' Aurora replied. '*I suggest you wake Pell now. We don't have long.*'

'That makes sense,' he agreed, 'but you avoided the real question.'

'Yes, I did, didn't I?' she said and promptly fell silent again.

Elian could tell he was going to get nothing further, so he did as he was told. He climbed to his feet and brushed the loose snow from his blankets before folding them and tucking them into his saddlebags. Stepping across to where Pell was gently snoring, Elian nudged him in the back with the toe of his boot. Pell went from totally asleep to completely awake in an instant.

'Wha . . .? What?'

'Time to get up,' Elian said tersely. 'Dawn is nearly on us. We need to be in the air when the sun breaks the horizon if we're to use the gateway.'

'Oh, the gateway,' he mumbled. 'Right!'

Even though he did not sound in the slightest bit convinced, Pell was quick to get up and start packing his gear. Elian had to give him credit for his motivation. Pell was clearly determined to get going early even though he must still be exhausted after the previous day's adventures.

As the fire had stayed alight through most of the night, there was enough heat in the embers to brew a hot drink before moving out from under the trees. The heat of the sweetened liquid was most welcome after such a freezing cold night and, despite not having slept, Elian felt remarkably refreshed by the hot liquid lining his stomach.

He and Pell stumbled out from under the snow-laden trees into the dim pre-dawn light. At some point in the early hours the snow had stopped. Elian had not noticed, as the wind had continued to stir the branches and shower him with loose snow every now and then. Out from the cover of the trees, the snow depth had increased significantly overnight. Within a few paces from the edge of the wood, Elian was knee deep. Rather than risk the uneven footing underneath the smooth white carpet, he waited until Aurora emerged from the trees and climbed onto her back.

'*Any sign of them?*' Elian asked again, not even daring to hope. He felt Aurora reach out with her mind, but he knew the answer before she vocalised it.

'*No. Nothing.*'

Pell was mounted on Shadow beside them.

'Let's get airborne,' Elian called. 'We'll see if there's any sign of the girls from the air and make a decision then.'

Pell shrugged. As far as Elian could tell, Pell did not care about the girls. He didn't get on with either of them, so he might be happy if they did not show up. Elian did not relish the idea of continuing the quest without the other two dragonriders, but he knew he would do what he had to, if only for Aurora's sake. This quest meant everything to her. He would not let her down.

Shadow leapt into a bounding run, hampered by the deep snow. With her huge wingspan she was able to power up into the air without too much difficulty, but Elian watched her with a certain amount of trepidation. Would his dragon, Aurora, be able to get up enough speed to get into the air?

'*Just watch me!*' she said in his mind, clearly eavesdropping on his thoughts again. '*Hang on tight, this could be interesting.*'

'Interesting' did not begin to describe it. Rather than running through the snow, her movement was more like a bounding gallop. The rhythm was most unusual and made staying on her back difficult. Elian bounced up out of the saddle with every leap, his bottom meeting the leather with a painful thump every time her forelegs hit the ground. Her wings extended and drove down hard in an effort to lift clear of the surface. On her first sweeping stroke, her wingtips caught the surface of the snow, causing her to tip forwards and hit the ground hard. Somehow she kept from falling forwards and continued bounding faster and faster.

The second stroke was more successful, pulling her up into the air. Another rapid beat and her trailing feet lifted clear of the snow. They were airborne and pumping upwards, settling quickly into a more familiar rhythm.

No sooner had Elian begun to relax into the saddle when his heart was set racing a second time.

'*Night dragons!*' Aurora warned suddenly, her voice loud in his mind. '*Segun and his dragon, Widewing, are coming with others. There are at least four of them and they're all coming this way.*'

Chapter Seven
Left Behind

'Have you sensed any sign of the others yet, Fire?' Nolita asked again, huddling down as best she could against Firestorm's back.

'Sorry, Nolita,' Firestorm replied, his tone glum. 'I must have picked a wrong valley earlier. Somehow we turned further left than I realised. When we came out of the mountains we were heading almost due north . . .'

'And the others were heading south,' Nolita finished.

Her heart sank as she considered the implications of having lost contact with the others. If she and Fire did not find them soon, she would be forced to spend a night alone with her dragon. The thought made her stomach churn. It was the strength and support of the others that had kept her going on the quest so far. Without them she was lost.

Nolita began to feel her old fears creeping out

of the dark corners of her mind. They were like sinister shadows lurking at the edge of her senses, waiting to pounce. Kira and Elian had encouraged and emboldened her more than she had ever thought possible. She did not want to think what it would be like without them now. For the first time since her brief trial at the day dragon enclave, she was alone with her dragon.

'Don't worry, Nolita,' Fire urged, sensing his rider's rising panic. 'We will catch up with the others, I promise. I will fly all night if necessary, but please don't be foolish about this. I don't want you to freeze to death. You don't need to stop long. I can light you a fire in seconds so you can get warm and we can move on.'

'Thanks, Fire,' Nolita replied, feeling genuinely touched. She paused. Firestorm was so caring, but she could not totally banish her fear of him. It was his size, nothing more. Knowing him intimately through the bond, she now accepted her fear was irrational, but even being convinced that he meant her no harm was not enough to banish the feelings.

'It's me who should be apologising,' she continued. 'I hope you understand. I know you'd never deliberately hurt me, but my fears will not go away. It doesn't make any sense, but I can't stop the feelings. That's just the way it is.'

'You have come further than you realise, dragonrider,'

he said, his tone flavoured with pride. '*I have watched you learn to control your fears in two short weeks. New circumstances inevitably cause them to flare. The fears have dominated your life for a long time, but I can see your bravery is more than a match for them. Be assured I will not test your strength unnecessarily, Nolita. We will press southwards and continue to look for the others as long as we can.*'

The light was fading and the snow showed no sign of letting up. The bitter cold had long since numbed the feeling in Nolita's toes, fingers and cheeks. Her fur-lined clothing had insulated her body against the worst of the wind chill, but they had been airborne for a considerable time now. Her body was cold-soaked and she knew she would have to land soon or risk permanent injury.

Visibility was very limited. Even during occasional lulls when the snow's intensity thinned, Nolita could see about a league at best. In the heavier bursts, she was unable to see more than a few hundred paces. The constant bombardment of snowflakes forced her to half close her eyes so that her lashes kept the flakes from blurring her vision. The fading light heralded the impending fall of night. It would not be long before the darkness effectively blinded her altogether.

When Fire made the link with Fang, Nolita felt

his surge of excitement and relief through the bond and guessed he had found at least one of the others. Her mirrored emotions were short-lived. Fire's thoughts moved instantly to urgent concern, bordering on panic.

'What is it? What's wrong, Fire?'

'It's Fang and Kira,' he answered, his mental voice sounding clipped in her mind. 'They're in trouble, but I can help. Hang on.'

Hanging on was not easy. With no sensation left in her fingers and her limbs weakened by hours of flying in the bitter cold, all Nolita could do was lean forwards and wrap her arms around the ridge in front of the saddle. Fire dipped into a shallow dive and began to drive forwards with all his might in an effort to reach Fang and Kira as quickly as possible. Nolita closed her eyes, feeling the wind rush increase as Fire accelerated through the blizzard.

'Brace yourself. We will land shortly,' Fire warned. 'Keep your head down. This will be like when we had to burn our way out of the wood, except this time we're going in.'

Nolita did not know how she could possibly brace herself any more, but she was glad of the warning. The abrupt change of speed and body angle was almost too much. If she had not known it was coming, the sudden deceleration and running landing would most likely have thrown her from the saddle. The abrupt strain as they landed made the muscles in her arms feel as if they were exploding as she fought to stay on Fire's back.

Fire slowed to a walk and Nolita felt his chest expand beneath her as he inhaled ready to breathe his hottest fire. Eyes closed, and half dangling by stirrups and arms, she wriggled backwards until she settled into her saddle. The rumbling roar of Fire's flame made her instinctively hold her breath. She expected him to pause before entering the trees, but he continued walking forwards into the burning path ahead.

The crackling of burning wood and the stinging smell of smoke filled the air. The reflected heat of Firestorm's torching breath was so hot that Nolita feared her numbed flesh might blister without her feeling the damage. He paused his deluge of fire and suddenly she could hear Kira's voice ahead.

'Kill them, Fire! Kill them all!'

She was hysterical! The shock of hearing the normally fearless huntress in such a state was enough to make Nolita risk opening her eyes. Firestorm drew another breath. Fiery twigs and charred pine needles were dripping from the trees around them in an orange and black rain. Smoke and steam filled the air, but Nolita could just see the outline of Fang through the swirling murk ahead. In the brief moments before Fire began spraying more bright flames from his mouth, she had time to make out what looked like dozens of ropes holding Fang in place. There was also a wide ring of red around him where his blood had stained the snow.

'What the . . .?' she spluttered.

A second roaring jet of fire sprayed from her dragon's mouth. He played it back and forth across the snow between them and Fang. To her amazement the snow did not just melt. It retreated in a wriggling mass of serpentine whiteness. She rubbed her eyes, thinking she was seeing things, but the rubbing made no difference. The squirming wave of white was definitely alive. Alive with what, she did not care to know.

Gradually, Fire breathed the flames closer and closer to Fang. Nolita no longer cared about burning embers. Her attention was focused on Kira and Fang. With startling abruptness, all the rope-like creatures released their grip on Fang and joined the multitude in the fast retreating wave. Fang opened his mouth and roared. Nolita could see he was still straining against something. The dusk dragon's muscles were bunching hard as he pushed up from the ground with all his strength. Quivering with the effort, he surged to his feet and turned. Another long line of the creatures was attached to his other side. Firestorm breathed more fire at them and they were quick to detach and snake away at an alarming speed to join the myriad others.

'Kira? Are you all right?' Nolita called anxiously.

'A lot better for seeing you and Firestorm,' she called back. 'If you hadn't come along, we would be dead for sure.'

'Is it safe to climb down, Fire?' Nolita asked.

'So long as you stay in the area I've cleared of snow, you will be perfectly safe,' he replied. *'The swarm won't venture onto the bare ground by choice.'*

Although she was tempted to ask him about the swarm, Nolita wanted to see Kira. She slid down Fire's side and hit the ground running. The earth steamed beneath her feet, still warm from Firestorm's torching breath. Kira was dismounting more slowly. As Nolita drew closer, her run faltered first to a stuttering walk and then to a complete stop. Fang was every bit as big as Firestorm. His looming presence set all the alarms going inside her head again. Her legs refused to take her any closer, so she waited.

Kira slid the last few hand spans to the ground and promptly collapsed, clutching at her right leg. Fixing her focus firmly on her friend, Nolita gritted her teeth and blanked the hulking presence of the

81

dusk dragon from her mind. Forcing her legs to move, she stumbled the final short distance to Kira's side. The Racafian girl was curled on the ground, sobbing. Nolita knelt down beside her and placed a hand on her shoulder.

'It's all right, Kira,' she said softly, her heart racing. 'It's all right. Fire will heal your leg. You'll be fine. Hush now. It'll all be all right. You'll see.'

Kira looked up at her, eyes filled with tears not just born of pain, but of anguish and guilt. 'I hesitated, Nolita,' she said. '*I* hesitated! I didn't do as Fang said and I nearly got us both killed. If you hadn't come along those ... those *things* would have eaten us and it would have been *my* fault.'

'You don't know that for certain, Kira,' Nolita protested. 'There were masses of them. Who's to say they wouldn't have pinned Fang down anyway? They must be strong to hold down a dragon. It looked to me as though flames were about the only thing that would shift them.'

'That's just it,' Kira sobbed, 'I couldn't even light a fire. What sort of a hunter can't light a fire? If I'd got a fire going, they probably wouldn't have come near us at all. I'm pathetic!'

'Nonsense!' Nolita said firmly, shocked to see Kira like this. 'You're one of the most capable people I know. It's freezing and you're from a tropical climate. What do you expect? Now stop running yourself down and let's get your leg sorted out. What were those things anyway? They looked disgusting.'

'Fang called them ice worms, and "disgusting" doesn't begin to describe them.' Kira shuddered and her eyes went distant. 'No eyes, a large mouth full of the most horrible teeth you've ever seen . . . and tough! I never realised something that size could be so difficult to kill.'

Firestorm was quick to breathe his healing fire over Kira. Nolita sat with her back to her dragon, but also in the flow of his amazing blue nimbus. A sense of warmth and well-being rushed through her as she sat with her friend. Her fatigue melted away and sensation returned to her fingers, toes, cheeks, nose and ears. Next to her, Kira sighed with relief as the pain in her leg first eased and then disappeared altogether. No sooner had her wound closed than she was on her feet and at her dragon's side.

Fang's healing was next. It took several breaths of the blue flames to heal all of the dusk dragon's injuries. There were dozens of nasty wounds in the underside of his body. Some of the ice worms had eaten right through his scales and deep into his flesh.

Nolita watched with mixed feelings as Firestorm

moved away. She was delighted to see Kira free from pain, but even with her friend at her side, Nolita was unable to totally banish the apprehension that she always felt in the presence of the dragons. When he walked away from her, she felt a sense of relief, but this time he did not go far. Fire took a few steps and grabbed a fallen pine trunk between his teeth. Although not fully grown, the tree was heavy. With a series of jerking movements that reminded Nolita of a dog pulling at a rope, he dragged the tree trunk into the centre of the area he had cleared of snow and then he snapped it neatly in two. Using his great talons with remarkable dexterity, he rolled the two halves together before setting fire to them.

As Firestorm moved away from the burning logs, Nolita and Kira moved closer to enjoy the generous heat they gave off. Nolita had felt so well after bathing in Firestorm's restoring breath, she was surprised at how tired she felt. It took a while for her to realise that this fatigue was not her own. It was coming through the bond. The healing fire of her dragon had revived her and her friends, but his efforts had left him exhausted.

'*Thanks, Fire. You were amazing. Now rest,*' she told him gratefully. '*You've earned it.*'

'*Thank you, Nolita,*' he replied. '*But we must not stop long. We have to find the others before dawn.*

Aurora's gateway to the other world will be a welcome sight at sunrise. Segun and his men cannot follow us there. It will be good to leave them as far behind as possible.'

They rested for just over an hour. The two girls sat quietly soaking up the heat from the fire and taking the opportunity to eat and drink. Occasional movements in the snow at the edge of the melted area niggled at the corners of their eyes to begin with, but it was not long before all fell still and silent aside from the gentle crackle of the fire.

The girls talked in low voices, and first Kira and then Nolita told of what had happened after they had split. Nolita told Kira about the fear she had experienced when she had thought she was going to spend the night alone with her dragon. Kira was a good listener and spending this time with her reminded Nolita how much she missed her older sister, Sable.

It was Firestorm who insisted they move again. The snow was still falling, as was the temperature.

'We cannot delay any longer,' he told Nolita. *'I sense night dragons approaching. They are still some distance away. I can't tell if they have located us yet, but if we stay here, they will find us for sure.'*

Nolita wasted no time. She was on her feet in an instant.

'Night dragons!' she said, grabbing Kira by the arm. 'We've got to go! Now!'

The two girls scrabbled to throw their things into bags and climb up onto their dragons. In little more than a minute they were on the move, taking the path that Firestorm had burned through the trees on his way in.

There was no sign of the ice worms as they made their take-off run through the deep snow outside the cover of the trees. Nolita was glad and Kira felt an even keener sense of relief. Launching into the darkness was less frightening to Nolita than in daytime. The lack of visual cues made flying easier to cope with.

No sooner were they airborne than they turned to the south, powering along at a frantic pace in an effort to slip away from the approaching night dragons. The fast rhythmic beating of the dragons' wings infected both girls with a breathless sense of urgency and a creeping anxiety that the night dragons would begin actively chasing them at any moment.

Nolita felt Fire reaching out frequently with his mind. He searched ahead for any sign of Aurora and Shadow, and then more tentatively behind them to try to discern if the night dragons were aware of them. As he said nothing, she remained content to concentrate on keeping her fear of flying under control by counting his wingbeats and keeping her eyes firmly shut.

On they flew, the relentless falling snow and bitter temperature gradually chewing through Nolita's thick clothing until once again numbness began to creep across her body. In subtle incremental shades the sky brightened in anticipation of the rising sun. Whenever she did briefly open her eyes, the snow-covered landscape below appeared a ghostly grey/white in the pre-dawn half-light. The spectral shadows and the hypnotic falling snow gave ample reason for Nolita to keep her eyes shut as much as possible.

'*More trouble!*' Firestorm's warning was preceded by a surge of emotion through the bond. '*I sense Shadow and Aurora ahead, but the main body of night dragons are there, too. They must have split up to search for us.*'

'What do you think we should do?' Nolita asked.

'*There is nothing we can do,*' Fire said, his voice sounding frustrated. '*They're too far away. We will not reach them in time. Aurora's forming a gateway. Segun is closing. She has no choice. Shadow's gone.*' He paused. '*Aurora's gone, too. They have left us behind.*'

Chapter Eight
Crash!

'Bloody hell!' Jack swore as a huge explosion lifted the tail of his aircraft, leaving it pointing almost vertically down at the ground. His ears rang with the aftershock of the noise as he wrestled with the controls, desperately trying to coax the machine back into level flight. He pulled back further and further on the yoke with little noticeable effect. The aircraft was accelerating towards the ground in a death dive.

A glance over his shoulder was enough to confirm the damage was bad. The tailplane was in tatters and there were gaping holes in the fuselage. His elevators were almost completely gone, leaving him with extremely limited pitch control.

'I'm damned if I'm going down in enemy territory,' he growled, pulling back the yoke as far as he could. 'Come on, baby! You can do it. Don't let me down now.'

The sound of the wind in the wires built rapidly from its normal whistling song to an unearthly howl as the aircraft plummeted towards the ground. The needle on the airspeed indicator cranked around rapidly, already exceeding the maximum recommended velocity. The aircraft was falling at a speed that Jack knew could tear the fabric apart ... and it was still accelerating.

Was this the end? Would all his combat experience be concluded by one lucky shot from the ground? It did not seem fair. Against all the odds, he had survived far longer than perhaps he deserved. He had gambled time and again during combat, but somehow he had always managed to return home in one piece. He had begun to feel almost invincible – a dangerous illusion that had claimed the lives of all too many of the flying aces.

'Oh no you don't,' he snarled at his machine, his teeth gritted and his lips pulled tight in a determined grimace. 'I'm not ready to die just yet.'

He could see the lines of the trenches ahead. If he could just flatten the dive sufficiently, he would at least impact the ground on friendly soil. Many pilots had miraculously walked away from crashes before. He just needed to give himself the best chance of survival. At least if he crashed on the right side of the lines and lived, he would not have to worry about being dragged off as a prisoner of war.

He suddenly realised that in the shock of the moment, he had not touched the throttle control, which was still in a cruise setting. He throttled it back to idle and instantly began to feel the slowing propeller act like an airbrake. The airspeed stabilised, still dangerously high, but no longer increasing.

'JUST A LITTLE HIGHER!' he yelled, releasing his frustration in a great shout. The muscles in his arms started to twitch with the effort of sustaining the pull force, but little by little the nose of the aeroplane began to climb, as the earth loomed closer and closer.

'How long have we got, Ra?' Elian called aloud.

'*Not as long as I'd like,*' she replied. '*It's not quite dawn yet. The barrier between worlds isn't weak enough to form a gateway. Besides, I don't want to use all my strength getting us there. I must be able to get us back again at the next opportunity.*'

'*What are you going to do?*'

'*Climb,*' Aurora said bluntly. '*The higher we can get, the closer to dawn we will be. Segun will expect* us to run, but I'm hoping he doesn't know about the gateways.'

'Surely Widewing will be able to out-climb us even if we get above her,' Elian pointed out, searching the sky above for signs of the incoming night dragons.

'Yes, but if we're quick, she won't reach us in time to prevent our escape.'

Elian clung tightly to the pommel grips as Aurora pounded the air with her wings, converting every possible scrap of energy into height. Shadow powered past them and climbed away at a seemingly impossible angle. If it had not been for the reported proximity of Segun and his lieutenants, Elian felt sure that Pell would have enjoyed showing off his dragon's superior strength.

'He's probably enjoying the moment regardless,' Elian muttered, grinding his teeth at the thought. 'Where are Segun and his cronies?' he asked Aurora silently, trying to shift his focus back to more practical thoughts. 'I can't see them anywhere.'

'Closing from our right,' she answered.

'Shouldn't we turn left to give them more of a chase?'

'If we were looking to drag out a long chase, then yes that would be logical,' Aurora admitted. 'But at the moment, Segun and his men are being very casual about the interception. They think they have us out-manoeuvred. If we turn away, they will almost certainly *accelerate to curtail the chase. I don't think we would gain anything other than to increase their focus. I want to keep them over-confident.'*

As they climbed higher the sky around them continued to brighten. The line of mountains towered to their right and Elian's excitement rose as he saw them catch the first direct rays of the sun. Dawn was close – really close. Almost at the same moment he noticed the movement in the corner of his eye. Four black dragons were closing fast from slightly above and to their right. Even as he looked, they began to turn and descend on a rapid intercept course. By Elian's best estimate, he and Pell had less than a minute before Segun and his men caught up with them.

'I've made contact with Fire,' Aurora announced suddenly.

Elian's heart leapt. 'Just in time!' he exclaimed, inadvertently speaking aloud in his excitement. 'Where is he? Are Fang and Kira with him?'

'Yes, Fire is flying with Fang, but they are too far away to be of help,' she replied. *'They are also too far away to reach us before the dawn window. I've told them to run for it. I don't think Segun is aware of them. He and Widewing are totally focused on us. We are going to leave without them.'*

'What? But we can't, Ra!' Elian protested. 'The

Oracle said we were to work together, remember? If we go through to the other world, they will never catch up with us.'

'I have not forgotten the Oracle's words, Elian,' Aurora said, her voice determined. 'But we have no choice. Segun is out for blood. If we lose this opportunity to slip through his fingers, he will not give us another. I have told Fire we will look for them "at the place where the shadows dwell," wherever that may be. We must hope for the Oracle to let slip another clue when we deliver the second orb. If any team can find the third orb, it will be Kira and Fang.'

Elian knew his dragon was right, but abandoning them here felt terrible. His chest tightened and a lump formed in his throat as he felt Aurora gathering her energy to form the gateway. Kira and Fang were the partnership most likely to outwit Segun and the night dragons, but he felt a certain sense of responsibility towards both of the girls.

Elian sensed the moment of dawn through the bond. It brought with it a surge of power that filled him with burning energy. Aurora's concentration was total. In the swirling snow ahead the familiar grey circle of swirling nothingness that led to the other world was barely visible. He heard Aurora's directions to Shadow as the bond between them momentarily swelled. In that instant of total openness, he shared her deepest thoughts. His heart pounded as he realised she was no more comfortable with leaving their friends behind than he was. Also there was the conviction that they had no choice. Elian's breath caught in his throat.

Shadow dived into the vortex ahead of them. A heartbeat before they followed, Elian glanced over his shoulder to see Segun on Widewing powering towards them, no more than a few dragon-lengths away. Even through the falling snow Elian could see his expression. The look of fury on his face was unlike any Elian had ever seen before – then he was gone. Grey limbo swallowed Elian. A brief feeling of weightlessness, then the twisting snap of emergence, followed the gut-wrenching twist of entry.

Aurora came out directly behind Shadow. Elian instantly looked back over his shoulder to see if Widewing had somehow entered the vortex, but the gateway had collapsed immediately behind them. If Segun and his dragon had entered the vortex, they had not made it through to the other side.

They had been out of the vortex just a few seconds when a barrage of explosions split the air around them with great roars. Puffs of smoke, some black and some white, marked each blast of sound and light.

'Shadow and Pell are terrified,' Aurora announced, sounding almost smug.

'I can't say I blame them,' Elian replied, his ears ringing and his heart thumping. 'Let's get out of here, Ra. Someone's directing those flash-bangs at us and I don't think they're meant as a friendly hello. They sound far more powerful than the stingers that hit you before. Also, if we're hit, we don't have the benefit of Firestorm's healing breath on hand. Let's not push our luck.'

'You are right, Elian,' Aurora agreed. 'Wait a moment, though!'

'What?'

'It's that man in the flying machine again,' she said, sounding almost irritated. 'It seems we can't avoid meeting him.'

'The same one again!' Elian exclaimed. 'Where?'

'Below and to the right,' she replied. 'And if I am not mistaken his machine is badly damaged. I believe he is going to crash.'

'Quick! Do something!'

'What do you suggest?' she asked. 'I can't catch something that big.'

'Maybe not,' Elian said quickly, 'but you might be able to pull him clear. We have to try something.'

There was an unspoken sense of 'why' from Aurora, but she did not argue. Instead she tipped into a dive and followed the stricken machine down. Elian ducked low to Aurora's back and concentrated on looking ahead at the airman's damaged machine.

There was little time for planning. They began their dive from about five hundred spans. The flying machine was already about one hundred spans below them, hurtling towards the ground. Its plummeting dive was gradually getting shallower, but it was not pulling out of the dive fast enough to prevent the inevitable impact.

Aurora folded her wings back and stooped like a gigantic hawk dropping to strike at fleeing prey. The ground swelled with frightening speed.

'*The man is strapped in,*' Elian realised. '*If you try to snatch him free, you might kill him. Try to grab the main wings of his flying machine from above and tip it into level flight.*'

Aurora did not reply, but Elian could feel his dragon's concentration as she closed rapidly on her target. They were running out of altitude. His mind flashed back to his fall from the Devil's Finger and her amazing coordination and skill in plucking him from the air. Now she struck, her talons tearing through the upper surfaces of the wings on either side of the cockpit. Elian felt her surge of panic as they ripped straight through without catching on anything of substance. Just when it seemed she had done nothing but damage the machine further, her rear-facing talons caught on something solid at the front of the wing. Snapping her own wings out to their full span, she heaved the front of the aircraft upwards until it was flying level. A warm sense of pride surged through Elian's chest. His dragon's timing could not have been better. As she let go, the machine was left skimming a few hand spans above the ground.

Aurora soared clear of the ground and high into the air and Elian looked over his shoulder anxiously to see the tattered machine touch down. It bumped and crunched to a most ungainly halt behind them. Allowing her momentum to carry her upwards until she was almost out of energy, Aurora dipped her left wing into a tight turn to bring her back around and down. She landed neatly next to the broken remains of the contraption's central body.

The flying machine was totally wrecked. The landing legs had gone. The whole tail section had detached, as had one of the main wings. Amazingly, however, the section in which the man was sitting remained virtually undamaged. A large shape swooped overhead and landed behind the remains of the machine. It was Pell on Shadow.

For a moment the man inside the machine sat still, apparently frozen by the shock of his crash. The familiar crack of a weapon stirred him into action. There was a whining sound as one of the stinging projectiles sang through the air. Several further loud reports sounded, and Elian flattened himself against Aurora's back. With impressive speed the man leaped out of his machine and sprinted the short distance to Aurora's side, head down and dodging randomly from side to side as he ran.

'Do you understand me?' the man said in a rush. His speech sounded strange, but Elian understood him perfectly.

'Just speak normally,' Aurora told Elian. *'I'll ensure he understands.'*

'Yes,' Elian told him. 'I understand.'

'We have to get away from here now,' he said, looking around frantically. 'We're between the lines. The men in the trenches on both sides are probably surprised and intrigued, but bullets are already beginning to fly. Please, can you carry me away from here? I need to get back into friendly territory.'

'Come. Climb up,' Elian said, automatically extending his hand. 'Use my dragon's foreleg. She won't hurt you. Hurry!'

The sound of weapons' fire in the immediate area died away and a peculiar feeling began to come over Elian. He was suddenly drawn to look across at Pell, who had climbed down from Shadow's back. Elian felt a strong urge to get down out of the saddle and cross the muddy ground towards Pell. What was it? The older boy looked extremely pale.

'Get away from here!' Pell yelled. 'Get away! The sun is setting. Get as far away as you can. It's begun. I can't resist it. The orb's pull is too strong.'

'Gods!' Elian breathed, suddenly realising what was happening. He had been so caught up in saving the stricken flying machine that he had not noticed the sun making its final dive towards the horizon. The airman, now halfway up Aurora's side, was also distracted by the pull of the orb. 'Quick!' Elian urged, yanking the man up into position behind him. 'We're in more danger than you can possibly imagine. Hold on to me. That's it. Now get us out of here, Ra – as fast as you can.'

Aurora needed no further encouragement. She raced across the mud and powered into the air, flying low over the trenches to the west, but gaining height with every wingbeat. Their prior knowledge of the orb's power allowed them to resist its subtle pull, but it was growing stronger by the second.

As they swiftly distanced themselves from the

orb, so the urge to return decreased. When the strange mental pull had reduced to nothing, Elian looked back over his shoulder. Far below he could just make out Pell. Lines of men were approaching him from east and west – lots of men, all walking with the same empty mindlessness. Elian turned away. From Pell's description of what had happened in the mountains, he knew what would come next.

Although he felt a morbid sense of curiosity, he had no desire to see them die.

Chapter Nine

Convergence

Segun was livid. Twice he had come close to claiming and destroying the dark orb. Both times it had slipped from his grasp. Prudence had made him step back the first time. If he had tried to take it from the plinth after his rider, Dirk, was exposed for cheating in the challenge, the griffins would have killed him. Nobody in their right mind crossed the griffins in their home territory. It had been frustrating to see Pell, the upstart young rider, fly away with it, but there had been no choice. Now the annoying brat had slipped away again.

'Tell everyone to land, Widewing,' he ordered silently, still contemplating the grey vortex that had swallowed the two dragons from under his nose. He had never had dealings with dawn dragons before. They had seemed insignificant – until now.

The vortex had formed at the instant of dawn. Whatever it was, it seemed likely that the dawn dragon had created it. *'The Great Quest must not be allowed to succeed, but it appears we're too late to stop the dark orb from reaching the Oracle. We must find another way.'*

Widewing did not answer, but she relayed the message without question. The four dragons descended in lazy circles towards the white fields below, Widewing leading the way. Segun rubbed at his tired eyes with the frozen fingers of his gauntlets. He felt weary. They had searched for the young riders all night. Now it appeared their efforts had been in vain. What should they do next? His frustration made him want to hit something. He settled for slapping at his thighs to stimulate blood into the numb surface flesh.

They landed. The snow was knee deep, but Segun kicked through it, channelling his anger into his legs and barely noticing the resistance. He crossed the short distance to where his fellow riders were gathering for a conference.

'Farvoice and Brighthorn are approaching from the north, Segun,' Widewing announced. *'Farvoice tells me they were following the trace of two dragons in our direction, but they have just lost contact. Do you think they were following the same two we flushed out?'*

'It seems likely,' Segun replied. '*Farvoice is sensitive to the presence of other dragon types. The distance seems extreme, but who knows what she is capable of? Tell them not to worry. They are to join us here as fast as possible. We have plans to make.*'

The four riders met in the open. Segun wasted no time with formalities.

'They are gone,' he said abruptly. 'Widewing sensed no trace of them once that strange grey cloud circle collapsed. Does anyone know anything of the capabilities of dawn dragons? What was that thing?'

'I've heard rumours that dawn dragons can open gateways between worlds, my Lord,' a rider responded. 'I'm told they're like portals.'

'So they are unlikely to return,' Segun sighed, not relishing the idea of a waiting game here in the exposed icy wastelands.

'No, my Lord,' the rider replied. 'Once in the other world a dawn dragon can open a return gateway to anywhere in Areth that they wish to go. They could be on the far side of the world by now.'

'Ah!' Segun said thoughtfully. 'Then it is easy to imagine where they might be. They will travel straight to the Oracle's cave. Thank you, Vikesh. If you are correct, this information will help us plan against their next move. Let me think.'

For the next minute he stamped in a small circle, trampling the snow until it was packed hard beneath his feet. When the circle was complete he looked back up at his men. They were standing awkwardly, shifting from one frozen foot to another and breathing steaming clouds into the snow-filled early-morning air.

'All right,' he said decisively. 'This is what we're going to do. Given what we know, I think it best to assume that Pell and his companions have now successfully recovered two of the orbs for the Oracle. We may have lost the dark orb, but that doesn't mean we can't stop them completing their quest. They still have two orbs left to find and we have the clue given to them by the griffins. "Seek the place where the shadows dwell." Does that mean anything to you?'

The three riders looked around at one another.

'Apparently not,' Segun observed, seeing their expressions. He drew a breath to continue.

'My Lord,' Vikesh interjected quickly. 'I've never heard of such a place, but I know where to begin the search.'

'Really? And where would that be?'

'The Grand Library in Harkesis, my Lord,' he said. 'It's said that the answer to every known question can be found there.'

Segun suspected there was not time to search a huge library for such an obscure reference, but there were many scholars at the library who could be paid to speed up the process. What was more, a trip to the city of Harkesis would not take them too far from his preferred course – a direct journey to the Oracle's cave.

'Thank you, Vikesh,' Segun replied thoughtfully. 'Good work. You can come with me and we shall try your idea. Cam – you and Nimred return to the enclave. Gather every dragon and rider you can find. I want the entire enclave to blockade the entrance to the Oracle's cavern. No one is to enter or leave that cavern without my say so. Is that understood?'

The two men nodded.

'The other enclaves won't like it. If they realise what we're doing, they may try to help the young-sters run the blockade. Don't waste time. Go now. We need every dragon and rider there as fast as possible. Do this right and the day dragons will not dare to come near. They're no fools. They'll not trigger a conflict they cannot hope to win. I'll be visiting the Oracle as well and I don't want to sit drumming my fingers waiting for you. Don't disappoint me, men.'

'No, my Lord,' they replied in unison.

'Widewing will order Farvoice and Brighthorn to continue the search for the other two missing dragons. It may be that they have already set out to find the third orb. Spread the word as you go that the night dragon enclave is offering two hundred gold pieces to anyone who supplies information resulting in our finding either of the remaining two dragon orbs. And offer a further hundred gold pieces to anyone who detains Pell, or any other rider seen consorting with him. It's unlikely that anyone will be able to do so, but it might slow our young friends down a little.'

'Consider it done, my Lord,' Cam replied.

The two men stomped back through the snow towards their dragons. Segun thought for a moment more, but there was little else he could do at the moment.

'Come, Vikesh,' he said. 'Let's ride for Harkesis and see if the scholars live up to their reputation.'

As soon as Fang told Kira that the boys had gone through a gateway, she knew what they had to do. Firestorm would stand out like a pig amongst goats if they stayed in the open. There was nothing else for it. With night dragons ahead and behind, they would have to turn right and slip back into the mountains to avoid being trapped.

'Close up to Fire,' she ordered. 'We must try to shield him with your camouflage. I doubt the dragons ahead have sensed us yet, but given the way the ones behind us have been following, I'm guessing they're on to us.'

'What have you got in mind, Kira?' Fang asked. 'None of the dragons can possibly see us in these conditions. They are too far back.'

'True, but Fire cannot shield his mind the way you can,' Kira explained. 'If you stay between Fire and the dragons behind us, I'm hoping that your ability will mask Fire from their senses enough to build confusion. As soon as we're close enough I want you to tell Fire to turn right. We're going back in amongst the peaks. It's our best chance.'

Fang had never thought of trying to shield another dragon in such a way before. He had done so physically, but never mentally. However, it made perfect sense. Without delay he slid in close behind Firestorm whilst employing his most intense physical and mental camouflage. He gave a quick explanation to the day dragon and then in a carefully coordinated manoeuvre, they turned. It was surprisingly difficult to do accurately, but as they changed direction Fang eased progressively around Fire, working hard to keep himself between the day dragon and the following night dragons.

They held the new course until the nearest mountainside suddenly reared out of the falling snow in front of them. The turn to avoid crashing into the mountainside was tighter, but no less coordinated. They went left until they were flying parallel to the slope and hugging the side of the mountain with Fang still maintaining the shield. As far as Fang could tell, the dragons behind had not changed course to follow them.

Minutes passed and a valley leading into the mountain range opened up to their right. They turned again, dipping into the valley and slowing. From the moment they entered the valley the wind drove the snow at them with increased fury. Visibility dropped still further, increasing the chance of crashing into an unseen mountainside.

'This is madness, Fang!' Kira told him. *'Fire can't possibly see where he's going in this. We need to find somewhere to land and hide out. Preferably somewhere that will offer us good shelter.'*

'I agree,' Fang replied. *'The night dragons are passing the valley entrance behind us and they are showing no sign of following. I believe we have lost them for now. It would be sensible to sit out the remainder of this storm somewhere safe and discuss our options. I will keep up the shield for a minute or two longer and then take the lead. My sense of sight is far keener*

than Firestorm's. Do not fear. I will lead us safely to shelter.'

Longfang was as good as his word. He took the lead and found a cave large enough to shelter both riders and dragons in little more than ten minutes. Once out of the snow, Firestorm heated some rocks with his fiery breath and the two girls recovered quickly, brewing hot drinks and cooking food to help speed the warming process. The cave was not very deep, so Fang positioned himself in the entrance and remained camouflaged, hiding the presence of the others.

Kira said nothing as Nolita heated a separate small pan of water with which to wash her hands and face. The proximity of Firestorm within the limited space of the cave made the blonde girl tauten. Kira knew that distraction was the most effective way to help her relax.

'Well, the boys are probably at the Oracle's cave by now,' she said, doing her best to sound positive. 'We'd better start concentrating on the next orb. I've been thinking about the dusk orb verse:

> *Ever protected, the dusk orb lies*
> *Behind the cover, yet no disguise.*
> *Afterlife image, unreal yet real,*
> *Lives in the shadows, waits to reveal.*

What do you think? Any ideas?'

Nolita's eyes were distant and she wrung her hands as if still rubbing soap into them. She did not answer for so long that Kira began to think she had not heard the question.

'I have one thought, but it's nonsense,' she said eventually.

'Nonsense? Ha! I doubt it's any worse than mine,' Kira replied. 'Go ahead. Try me.'

'It's the line "Afterlife image, unreal yet real",' Nolita said slowly. 'I can't get the idea out of my head that an afterlife image is a ghost. I don't believe in ghosts, but no matter how hard I try to twist the meaning around, I can't come up with anything else that fits the description.'

'That's exactly what I was thinking,' Kira said thoughtfully. 'Unreal . . . yet real. Does that mean ghosts are real? I don't know. Someone seeing the Oracle for the first time might consider it a ghost. It looks unreal, yet it's definitely real. If we accept the Oracle is real, then why not another form of spirit creature?'

'A spirit creature sounds better than a ghost to me,' Nolita admitted. 'Yes. A spirit creature that lives in the shadows. That makes sense. But where would you find such a creature?'

'In the place where the shadows dwell,' Kira

replied. 'The verse says "Lives in the shadows" and the griffins told us to look for "the place where the shadows dwell". I've never heard of anywhere that sounds like that. Have you?'

'No,' said Nolita, shaking her head. 'So where do we start looking? Look – we're in a cave. We're sitting in the shadows. Does this make the cave a place where shadows dwell? Clearly not, or the orb could be in any one of a thousand places. There must be somewhere special. Somewhere that is identifiable as the place where shadows live – a place where a spirit creature lives.'

They both fell silent. Where would they find such a place? It could be just about anywhere in Areth. It was Longfang who interrupted Kira's thoughts to offer a solution.

'*What about the Grand Library of Harkesis?*' he suggested.

'The Grand Library of Harkesis?' she said aloud for Nolita's benefit. 'I've never heard of it. Do you know of a spirit creature living there, Fang?'

'No,' he sighed. '*The Grand Library of Harkesis is the largest collection of information in Areth. If the answer to the Oracle's riddle has been written down, you will find it there.*'

'That makes sense,' Kira said thoughtfully. 'But there will be so much to read and we don't have much time. How will we find what we want to know?'

'*Ask one of the librarians to help you,*' Fang suggested. '*Many are scholars in their own right and will know where to look.*'

'All right, Harkesis it is,' she announced, meeting Nolita's eyes and giving her an encouraging smile. 'So where exactly *is* Harkesis?'

Chapter Ten

What's the Connection?

Jack was having trouble taking it in. He was flying on a dragon's back. It was a surreal experience.

His previous encounters with the dragons had always felt dreamlike. After his first sighting, he had wondered if the stress of combat was getting to him. Then there had been the fight when the dragons had destroyed three enemy aircraft. No one else had witnessed them tear those aeroplanes to pieces. His superiors had thought him delusional and sent him home on leave after his report on the incident, but they had been forced to change their tune after his last experience.

Jack had been on an extraction mission, picking up a French secret service agent from behind enemy lines when he had encountered the creatures again. He had been reluctant to mention the dragons in this second report, but the French spy was difficult to keep quiet on the subject. Only when Jack's Squadron Commander warned him that the dragons were a Top Secret project did he calm down. It had proved a good ruse to keep the man quiet.

Jack had seen only two dragons this time. And there was no sign of the girl. Her dragon had made itself invisible. Could she make herself invisible too? There was no telling what strange abilities these people had.

They flew west until they were clear of the battle lines and then they flew in gentle circles, apparently waiting for the second dragon and rider to catch up. Jack wondered what they were doing back in dangerous no-man's land. Perhaps they had been killed, though Jack felt this unlikely. Bullets had not penetrated the scales of the dragons before. It seemed their scales were formed of a material far tougher than anything the British Government had been able to develop.

Jack reached down and ran his fingers across one of the dragon's scales. It felt surprisingly soft and warm. How could something so soft turn aside bullets? There were so many questions to ask.

At last, the other dragon rose from the ground to join them and once again they flew westwards, away from the battle lines and deeper into friendly territory. Jack began to relax and enjoy the sensation of flying on this enormous creature's back. After so many flying hours spent inside the cramped cockpit of fighting machines, it was a delight to stretch his legs and enjoy the ride.

The light was fading fast now that the sun had dipped below the horizon. However, as the dragons began to descend, Jack suddenly realised where they were heading. He knew he should not interfere, but the riders had just saved his life. It did not feel right to let them fly into a trap.

Jack tapped the shoulder of the boy in front of him.

'You're going to the burnt wood, aren't you?' he said. 'Don't. People have been watching it since last year when all the local dogs went mad and your dragon burned a path through the trees. My Squadron Commander asked me about it because he thought I might have more information.'

'Last year? But . . . never mind. Thanks for the warning,' the boy replied over his shoulder. His eyes went distant for a moment before re-focusing. 'My dragon has confirmed it. There are watchers. We'll find somewhere else. Have you got any suggestions?'

Jack thought for a moment. There was a decent stand of woods not far from the airstrip his squadron were using. So long as they approached low and from the west, it was unlikely anyone would see them coming. He knew he would probably get into trouble for this, but he didn't care.

'Yes,' he said. 'I know a place where you can land in secret. It would be best if you told the dragons to go invisible.'

'Only Kira's dragon has the ability to camouflage himself,' the boy replied. 'And Kira's not with us. It's getting dark. We'll just have to be as careful as we can.'

It took about fifteen minutes to reach the woods. Judging by their apparent speed the dragons flew faster than his old scout aircraft. Aurora and Shadow landed and the riders dismounted. The dragons headed for the cover of the trees. As they followed the great creatures, Jack got his first proper look at the two boys. The one he had flown with looked no more than about fourteen. The other was older, possibly sixteen or seventeen. They both seemed far too young to be involved in secret projects, so it was unlikely the dragons were a part of any secret government plan – not that he had ever believed that story.

Jack turned to the younger boy and lifted his flying goggles from his eyes so that he could see him more clearly. 'Thank you,' he began. 'You have an uncanny way of turning up at just the right moment. I'm Jack – Jack Miller.' He held out his hand. After the slightest of pauses, the boy grasped and shook it.

'Elian,' he responded. 'And my companion is Pell. I've noticed that almost every time I've come through a gateway you seem to be nearby, and danger is never far behind you. Aurora, my dragon, says our destinies are intertwined. I don't know exactly what that means, but perhaps if we talk for a bit, we might work it out between us.'

'You speak English,' Jack noted. The girl rider he met before had spoken English as well. 'Where do you come from? Your accent is strange. I can't place it.'

'Actually I don't speak your language at all,' Elian said. 'My dragon is translating for us. Don't ask me how she does it, because I have no idea. I say something in my language and your mind hears it in your language. That's as much as I can tell you. It's the same in reverse for me. We don't come from your world, so your language is alien to us.'

Jack's mind spun as he tried to imagine how such instant translation worked.

'So when I've seen you disappear into those swirling grey cloud things, you were travelling to this other world?'

'Going back to it,' Elian answered. 'My dragon is a dawn dragon. She has the power to open the gateways, but only at the moment of dawn. We travel through your world in order to cover vast distances in our own.'

'You don't use the gateways very often then,' Jack observed.

'Well, we've used them a lot recently, but time doesn't move at the same rate here as it does in our world.'

'Time ... doesn't ...' Jack repeated slowly. His words petered out as he tried to imagine what the boy was talking about. Accepting that the dragons were coming from another world was hard enough, but time not moving at the same rate? That was not only impossible, it was beyond comprehension!

'How long has it been since we helped you collect your companion from that field?' Elian asked.

'The pick-up mission? Oh, ages! It seems like for ever ago now. That was back in February,' Jack said quickly, his mind racing through a quick calculation. 'About seven months.'

'I thought as much. For me it's only been a few days since that happened. In fact it's only been a couple of weeks since you first saw us take off from the field where your flying machine was housed.'

'But that was over a year ago!' Jack exclaimed. 'How can that be?'

'I don't know,' Elian admitted. 'My dragon tells me that the relationship between time in our two worlds is not linear. I'm not sure what that means, but time is currently moving much faster here than it is in my world.'

Jack thought for a moment. The boy appeared genuine. But the older boy, Pell, had said nothing. Throughout the conversation he had stared straight ahead, apparently unhearing and uncaring. It looked as if he was in a severe state of shock after his experience of no-man's land.

'I don't want you to get the wrong idea about me, but I think I should tell you that my superiors want you to help us win the war we're fighting,' he began slowly, remembering the communiqué he had received from the General after his last report. 'Your dragons appear immune to our weapons. The Generals would give a lot to have you on our side. I'm supposed to use whatever means possible to get you involved as our allies.'

Elian stopped walking and turned to face Jack in the fading light under the trees.

'Is that what *you* want, Jack?' he asked bluntly. 'We don't use the gateways by choice. We're involved in a dangerous quest. We've got precious little time to complete it and without using the gateways it would become impossible. To be honest your world scares me silly. I can't imagine what caused your people to begin fighting on such a massive scale and I don't want any part in it.'

Jack nodded. 'I don't blame you,' he said. 'Only a fool would get involved in a war that wasn't his own. This war has dragged on for years. The propaganda would have us believe we're winning, but I'm not convinced. These past months the Germans have been all over us in the air. Their tactics have been superior and it's hard to see what we can do to turn the tide. What I don't understand is why you keep appearing and helping *me*. You talk of destiny. Is there something you want in return?'

The two dragons had found places where they could lie comfortably between the trees. Elian did not answer straight away, but continued walking until he was alongside his dragon. He had the far away look in his eyes that Jack had noticed when they were in the air. Then it struck him. The boy was communicating directly with his dragon by a kind of mental link. If the dragon could mess with their minds to make the boy and Jack understand each other, then why should the boy not talk directly to his dragon's mind?

'Our two dragons alone wouldn't make much of a difference here, Jack,' Elian told him. 'Your war is beyond our ability to end. But you might be able to help us. Have you ever heard of a place where shadows dwell? Or anything about a dragon orb?'

Neither question meant anything to him. Jack shook his head.

Elian shrugged and then rubbed his hands together to warm them. It was getting cold now the darkness was setting in.

'Aurora feels you must be tied up with our quest somehow,' Elian said, puzzled. 'The gateways keep opening near you. But what's the connection?'

Jack watched the boy as he concentrated on the conundrum. He looked serious beyond his years. Was it normal for youngsters in the world of dragons to embark on dangerous quests?

'Perhaps I could help if I knew a bit more about this quest,' he said. 'What is a dragon orb?'

With a suddenness that startled him, Pell spun round, a look of unbridled fury on his face.

'You don't want to know about dragon orbs!' the older boy spat. 'They're cursed. Death and misery follow them. The sooner I get rid of the dark orb, the better.' As abruptly as his hostile outburst began, Pell's focus disintegrated again and his voice became distant as he continued. 'It's killed too many. Maybe Segun was right in wanting to destroy it.'

'We'll reach the Oracle tomorrow, Pell,' Elian told him soothingly. 'Don't worry. The orb has claimed its last victim.'

'So many . . .' Pell continued, showing no sign of having heard Elian. His eyes stared into space and tears rolled unchecked down his cheeks. 'So many men. Young and old. It killed them all. So many . . .'

Elian drew Jack away, leaving Pell next to his dragon. He was muttering incoherently now. Jack had seen the reactions of enough newly arrived pilots, fresh to the horrors of battle, to recognise the look in his eyes. The boy looked on the edge of losing his sanity.

They moved a short distance away and Elian began to speak in a low, urgent voice.

'Our quest is to find four dragon orbs and use them to restore a spirit creature known as the Oracle,' he said. 'We have found two so far, but each has harboured a danger that has taken us by surprise. The first caused the incident you referred to last year with the dogs. Pell has recovered the second, but it has a deadly quality unlike anything I've ever seen. Immediately after we flew away from your broken machine the orb killed many men on both sides of the battle lines. I expect someone will soon link these deaths to sightings of our dragons and you'll be asked more questions. Please believe me, we don't come here to cause harm. We're just travelling through.'

'How did it kill them?' Jack asked, instantly wondering if this orb could be used as a weapon.

'We don't know and we don't want to know. We just want to get it to the Oracle before it kills again. It's deadly.'

'So why don't you go now?'

'I told you,' Elian said patiently. 'We have to wait until dawn when my dragon can open another gateway.'

Jack fell silent. It was a lot to take in. Dragons, deadly dragon orbs, gateways to another world that only opened at dawn – it sounded like something from a fairy story. However, he could not deny the reality of it all. He had just flown here on a dragon's back. That was an experience he would never forget.

It was hard to know what to believe. Jack had never believed in God, yet there had been times in the air when he had prayed ... just in case. He had even muttered a 'thank you' on occasion, after particularly close encounters with death. The dragons and their riders had acted like guardian

123

angels on three separate occasions, arriving in the nick of time to save his life. Coincidence? It seemed highly improbable. They claimed they had no control over when they arrived, and that they were not deliberately opening their gateways near to him. If they were not doing it, who was?

He felt a strange connection with Elian and a prickle ran up and down his back as he accepted this fact. Was there such a thing as predestination? Had some higher force already mapped out his life? This scary thought made him want to know more.

'Elian,' he said aloud. 'Tell me more about this quest you're on. I want to know as much as you can tell me.'

Chapter Eleven
Harkesis

It had taken three-and-a-half days of hard flying, but when the city of Harkesis finally came into view the sight of it took Kira's breath away.

'Gods alive!' she thought, directing her exclamation through the bond to her dragon. 'It's huge!'

'I imagine the High Lord of Harkesis will be pleased by your reaction, Kira,' Fang said, his voice sounding amused.

Kira laughed aloud. 'And why would the High Lord care what I think?' she asked.

'The people of Harkesis are very proud of their city, and none more so than the High Lord,' Fang replied, his tone turning serious. 'You are a dragonrider. The dragonrider community wield a lot of influence across Areth. Your opinion is more sought after than you might imagine. Do not be surprised if you are invited to attend the High Lord's court while we are in Harkesis. It is a courtesy often extended to riders.'

'But I don't know the first thing about how to behave in a nobleman's presence,' she said, horrified by the thought of being expected to mix with the aristocracy.

'You will do fine, Kira,' Fang told her. 'If an invitation is extended, I will guide you through the experience. The courtesies required are not too difficult here.'

The bright white of the city buildings sprawling across the two coastal hills was reminiscent of the snowy mountains the girls had left behind. They stood out amongst the lush green of the countryside and against the bright blue backdrop of the eastern end of the Capsian Sea. Numerous buildings of all shapes and sizes covered the hillsides and flooded the valley between, but rather than being set in ordered rows, there was a chaotic look to the city's construction. The only consistent element was the colour – every building was as white as purest porcelain.

'Can you see the large building on the summit of the hill to the left?' Fang asked.

'Yes.'

'That's the library.'

Even though they were still leagues from reaching the edge of the city, Kira could appreciate the scale of the Grand Library building. It was an enormous structure: rectangular, but with a roof that sported five huge domes and high minarets at each corner that reached into the sky with needle-sharp points. There was no other building in the city that came close to matching it for size, or elaborate architecture.

'I assumed that was the High Lord's palace,' she admitted. 'I'm amazed that a library is the largest building. There are only two books in our tribe and both belong to the medicine man. One is a book of herb lore and the other is a collection of stories from the tribe's history.'

The thought of the storybook instantly brought memories flashing back through her mind. Only a very few people were taught to read in her tribe. It was not a skill that had much application to everyday life in the savannah. Every rainy season the Chief's wife would borrow the book of stories from the medicine man and read them to the younger children.

Kira remembered those days with a special fondness. The stories were colourful and exciting, and the Chief's wife read them with passion. The debates afterwards on the morals of the tales were always lively and Kira had enjoyed vivid dreams for many days afterwards.

'Learning is of primary importance to the people

of Harkesis,' Fang told her. 'The Grand Library has given the city a reputation for being the seat of learning in Areth. People travel here from all over the world to find answers to their questions. Even the lowest street urchins pride themselves on the combined knowledge of those within the city.'

'Any sign of night dragons?' she asked.

There was a pause as he searched ahead with his mind.

'No. None,' he said.

'Good.'

They flew on, angling towards the Grand Library and slowly descending until they were level with the hilltop on which it stood. As they swept in over the city, a closer view of the buildings dispelled the earlier image of purity. All of the houses had been whitewashed, but even from a hundred spans up, Kira could see the ramshackle construction of the tiny box-like hovels and the filth on the streets. Once they were over the city proper, Kira could smell it as well. The stench created by inadequate sanitation mushroomed up in a great bubble.

'How can they live amongst that?' Kira asked, horrified. She covered her mouth with her sleeve, gagging at the ripe aroma. Nolita, who was flying alongside her on Firestorm, was also filled with disgust.

'They become hardened to it,' Fang explained, sounding matter-of-fact. 'Smell something for long enough and eventually you will stop noticing it. At the moment the weather is stable and the pressure is rising. This makes the air descend, trapping the smell of the streets and allowing it to intensify. The people who live here are grateful for days when the air is less stable, or when there is a stiff breeze blowing.'

'But what makes so many people want to live here in the first place?' she asked. 'How do they find food? Surely the countryside has been stripped of game with so many people to feed.'

'They live here because they feel it brings them status.' Fang sounded contemptuous of the idea. Kira found her own emotions mirroring those of her dragon. 'The academics have found solutions to the problems of food and water. They have developed a clever system of intensive farming that produces far more food than the land would normally yield. What they cannot grow, they buy through traders. It is a complex system.'

'Sounds like madness to me,' Kira observed. 'What if the trade routes were disrupted? The city would starve.'

'It would not be the first time such a thing has happened,' Fang said sadly. 'Wealth is relative. Who is better off: a dragon with a comfortable cave and a *mountain of gold, or a dragon with nowhere to shelter, but who has a ready supply of fresh meat? The correct answer will depend on the circumstances.'*

Kira fell silent and surveyed the city with a mixture of wonder and disgust as the ground ahead rose towards the enormous structure perched on its peak. The courtyard in front of the Grand Library was a perfect square. The colonnade around its perimeter was topped with a string of eight small domes on each side, and was supported by delicate arches of pure white stone.

The enclosed area was large enough for the two dragons to land safely, though they had to slow to a brief hover before touching down to avoid inadvertently hurting anyone. A large number of scholars were milling in the courtyard as they approached. They scattered like frightened sheep at the sight of the dragons.

Fang landed with delicate precision in front of the great marble steps leading up to the gigantic main doors. Firestorm touched down with equal finesse alongside him. Both dragons folded their wings back and dipped down on their forelegs to allow the two girls to dismount.

Sliding down to the ground, Kira stepped smartly away from Fang and leapt up the first two enormous marble steps where she met Nolita. The blonde girl looked nervous, though it was not clear if this was due to the proximity of the dragons, or the imposing nature of the building in front of them.

'This way, Nolita,' Kira said in a low voice, trying to sound confident. 'Let's get this over with. I can't say I care much for the smell around here.'

She led the way up the remaining five steps to the threshold to the open doors. Towering pillars on either side of the doorway made for a most impressive entranceway. The twin open doors into the Grand Library were at least six times a man's height. They were carved from thick pieces of solid hardwood that had been so cleverly joined that they appeared to have been cut from a single, impossibly large tree.

Distracted by the sheer scale of the entranceway, Kira did not notice the man standing inside the doors until he spoke.

'Hello, dragonriders. I am Kalen. Welcome to the Grand Library. What can I do for you today?'

The man was a picture of wisdom: clean-shaven, pale and wrinkled with age, but with bright blue eyes that danced with intelligence. His full crop of silver hair was trimmed neatly around his ears and neck. His pale cream scholar's robe was clean and cinched at the waist by a belt of purple. What drew Kira's eyes most, however, was the way that the

131

man's head jutted forwards from his shoulders. It took a moment for her to realise that the man's spine was deformed. It looked almost as if his neck were broken, as his head tipped forwards at a strange angle, forcing him to look up at them through the tops of his eyes.

She stammered as she tried to respond with suitable poise.

'Hello, Kalen. I am Kira and this is Nolita,' she said. 'We're here seeking the answer to a riddle. I wonder if you can help us.'

'A riddle!' he said, sounding both surprised and delighted. 'A riddle whose solution escapes the wisdom of dragons must be a riddle indeed! I shall be honoured to help you. Come inside and tell me about it. I confess, I'm most intrigued.'

'Are you sure?' Kira asked, uncertain. How could she be sure he was the right person to ask for help? 'I wouldn't want to distract you from your work.'

'Not at all, Kira. I only take a turn in the doorway to allow me some space to think. It's always a pleasure to help dragonriders.'

'*From what I sense of his mind, he is genuinely interested in helping us, Kira,*' Fang told her, feeling her indecision through the bond. '*I think you can trust him. Firestorm and I are going to leave the courtyard and go down to the sea. We want to take the*

132

opportunity to bathe in the cool water. We will return for you in a couple of hours, or if we feel any night dragons approaching.'

'That's fine, Fang,' she replied. 'We'll see you later. Hopefully we'll have more of an idea of where we're going by then.'

Kalen gave a hand signal, and two young men in robes tied with yellow belts came running across from the colonnade to their right. The men leapt up the marble steps, keeping a good distance from the dragons. Fang and Firestorm launched into the sky and all the scholars who had hidden under the covered walkways were quick to step out to watch the two great creatures climb away.

Kira smiled at their reaction. It was clearly not an everyday occurrence for dragons to visit. The old scholar gave a brief set of instructions to the two juniors in a quiet voice and then gestured for Kira and Nolita to follow him inside.

'Excuse me, Kalen ... sir,' Nolita stammered as they crossed the threshold. 'Is there somewhere I could wash my hands?'

'Yes, of course!' Kalen said, looking particularly pleased. 'It's wonderful to see that you observe such customs. We normally require everyone to wash their hands before entering the Grand Library. Some of the books are priceless. It would be a disaster to have them ruined with dirty finger marks. I was going to waive protocol in your case, as you've clearly been wearing gloves, but I would feel much more comfortable if you washed your hands before entering. Through that door over there you will find basins with clean water and plenty of soap. The water boys change the basins twice every hour. The last change was completed just moments before you arrived.'

Kira knew that Nolita's request to wash had nothing to do with the books, but Kalen did not need to know that. He had pointed to an ordinary-sized side door set in the wall of the foyer. The girls went through it and found lines of bowls filled with clean water. A small block of soap rested in a dish next to each bowl.

Kira picked a bowl and gave her hands a cursory wash before drying them on a piece of soft dry cloth hanging on a wall hook just above the bowl. Nolita took considerably more time, scrubbing fiercely at the skin and cleaning thoroughly between her fingers and under her nails.

'Is it getting any easier?' Kira asked her as she waited. 'Do you feel as if you're coming to terms with being a rider yet?'

Nolita did not look up.

'No,' she said bluntly. 'I don't think I'll ever get

used to it. I thought the feelings of fear would reduce, but there doesn't seem to be any sign of that happening yet. I still find it as difficult to climb onto Fire's back as I did in the day dragon enclave. I am coping . . . just, but I don't think the fear will ever go away.'

'I sort of assumed—' Kira started.

'Well you assumed wrong,' Nolita interrupted. She looked up at Kira with the fire of anger in her eyes. 'It's not getting any easier. If anything it's getting more difficult. At the moment I cope because I have to – because there is a purpose behind what we're doing. But succeed or fail, this quest will be over in a few weeks and what then? You, Elian and Pell will go your own ways. I will be left with Fire – alone. Just the thought of that scares me more than anything I've ever known.'

'But Fire will never hurt you,' Kira said gently. 'You know that, don't you?'

'Understanding it, and making my heart and mind believe it are very different things,' Nolita sighed. 'I *know* it doesn't make any sense. I *don't know* why I'm still so afraid, but I *am*. There doesn't seem to be anything I can do about it.'

Kira placed a sympathetic hand on her shoulder. 'We'll work something out, Nolita. You'll see.'

The words were well meant, but Kira realised

how hollow they must sound. Nolita was right. The quest would end soon, one way or another. At the moment she could not imagine life after searching for the dusk orb. This was her part in the quest and it required focus. Danger had dogged their steps throughout. Nolita had completed her part. It was no wonder she was starting to look ahead and worry.

The girls rejoined Kalen and he led them deep into the Grand Library building. The short hallway ended with another set of impressive doors. These were a third of the size of the outer doors, but again had clearly been crafted with great skill. Kalen opened the right-hand door and waved the girls through ahead of him.

Kira gasped with wonder as she stepped into the vast room beyond. Her mind instantly flashed back to the Chamber of the Sun Steps at the enclave of the day dragons, and how she had felt as she entered that enormous cavern. If anything, this room was even more awe-inspiring than the volcanic cave because it was the work of human hands.

The circular walls of the vast space had five levels of balcony walkways running around its circumference, with sets of steps zigzagging up through the levels. What made the room dizzying, however, was not its size, but the incredible number of books that lined its walls. Every inch of space on the huge circular walls was shelved and each shelf was full of books.

The central area of the chamber was given to more bookcases. It looked like a maze. The huge, imposing bookcases interlocked in a complex geometric pattern to make maximum use of the ground-level floor space.

'Impressive, isn't it?' Kalen said in a low voice. 'There are four more rooms like this, but they are smaller. This is the central chamber.'

'I didn't know there were this many books in the world,' Nolita whispered.

Kira glanced across at her wide-eyed companion and then at Kalen. Nolita had echoed Kira's thoughts word for word. The man smiled.

'The problem with having such a wonderful library,' he said in a conspiratorial whisper, 'is that to be anyone in this city, you need to have written a book that is deemed worthy of a place in it.'

'So have you written a book that can be found here?' Kira asked.

Kalen's smile stretched wider still. 'Yes indeed – nine volumes now, with another that is currently being read by the Council of Librarians.'

'Nine books! That's amazing. I couldn't think of enough words to fill one book, let alone nine.'

'Writing is not so different from speaking, really,' Kalen said, trying to sound modest and not quite succeeding. 'Everyone knows enough words to fill a book. There are some who discover new things that add to the pool of human understanding. Others write of life experiences, or stories that encapsulate lessons designed to help people live better lives. It is developing the discipline to sit and string the words together in a way that brings something fresh and beneficial to literature that takes practice.'

'I can relate to what you're saying,' Kira admitted. 'Learning to be a hunter is similar. Everyone knows the basics: you go into the wild, you kill animals and you bring them back home for the table. It sounds easy, but to be any good at it takes years of practice.'

'An interesting analogy,' Kalen said thoughtfully. 'I've never heard anyone relate writing a book to hunting before. But now come, tell me your riddle and we'll see if I can help you find an answer.'

Chapter Twelve
'The Oracle Will Pay'

'There is something about this rhyme that's niggling at me,' Jack muttered. He scratched at his right ear, his forehead lined with wrinkles as he narrowed his eyes and concentrated. He stared at the words of the Oracle's poem. He had written them out on the back of his map so he would not forget them. The words made no sense.

> *Beyond time's bright arrow, life-saving breath,*
> *Love's life-force giving, slays final death.*
> *Orbs must be given, four all in all.*
> *Orbs to renew me, stilling death's call.*
>
> *Delve 'neath the surface, life's transport hides,*
> *Healing, restoring — bright river tides.*
> *Enter the sun's steps; shed no more tears.*
> *Attain ye the orb; vanquish the fears.*

Release the dark orb — death brings me life.
Take brave ones' counsel, 'ware ye the knife.
Exercise caution, stay pure and heed,
Yield unto justice: truth will succeed.

Ever protected, the dusk orb lies
Behind the cover, yet no disguise.
Afterlife image, unreal yet real,
Lives in the shadows, waits to reveal.

Life after death from death before life,
Enter the new age, through deadly strife.
Greatest of orbs is — dragon's device.
Gifted for ever: life's sacrifice.

'Does any of it make sense?' Elian asked, intrigued by Jack's reaction to the Oracle's riddling words. 'Given that we've now discovered the meanings of the verses that relate to the first two orbs, I expected to decipher the last two more easily, but they remain a mystery.'

'Sense? No,' Jack answered, shaking his head. 'But there's something about the poem ... something that tells me I can answer the riddles. Perhaps I am linked to your quest after all. It's like looking at a crossword. Some days you can look at the cryptic clues and the answers jump out at you.

Other days it doesn't matter how hard you look, the answers won't come, yet they are no more difficult. I'm having one of those frustrating days when the answers won't come, but I know they will. I *know* they will.'

Elian had no idea what a crossword was, but he got the sense of what Jack was saying. It was as he had suspected from the beginning. This man held the key to their quest. He could solve the final riddles. Even if he did not do it overnight, he could do it eventually.

With the answers to the riddles, the quest would become far easier. Once they knew where to look, it would be about tackling the challenges that waited at each orb's location. What test awaited him? he wondered. Just thinking about the question sent a shiver down his spine. Both Nolita and Pell had faced terrible trials to obtain their orbs. What would getting his orb involve?

The griffin, Karrok, had told them to seek the place where the shadows dwell, which was no doubt the location of the dusk orb. The verse relating to the dawn orb, however, gave virtually no clue to its whereabouts. Any help from Jack would be most welcome.

'That's great, Jack,' Elian said enthusiastically. 'Can I ask you a favour?'

'Go ahead,' he replied warily.

'Promise me you won't get yourself killed before you find the answers.'

Jack laughed. 'I'll do my best,' he said. 'The worst thing about this war is that it's so damned dangerous! People will insist on shooting at me every day. I suppose it is only fair, given that I shoot at them, but it's dashed antisocial, if you ask me.'

The night passed quickly, although none of them slept. Elian was alternately worried about Pell and fascinated by Jack's stories of the war. Jack, in turn, was eager to hear about Areth and its inhabitants. He was particularly interested in everything Elian told him about the dragons, the Oracle, the orbs and the griffins – those things he described as fantastical creatures. His eyes went wide when Elian told him the griffins had originated in his world, but had been taken to Areth by a dawn dragon centuries earlier.

As dawn approached, Elian felt a wave of fatigue crash over him. He desperately needed sleep, but it was far too late for that now. Pell had said next to nothing all night. His eyes were vacant. Dark rings under them added to his haunted expression. And his dragon looked little better.

'*The sooner we get Pell to the Oracle, the better, Ra.*'

'I agree,' she replied. 'Both Pell and Shadow are close to the edge of insanity. I would not have thought a night dragon could be affected by death in such a way. The dark orb must be a heavy burden. We have to get them to the Oracle with all haste.'

Elian gave Jack a quick wave goodbye as he settled into the saddle. The pilot raised a hand in acknowledgement, watching them from the edge of the woods as they prepared to leave. He appeared sad. The sky was brightening quickly in the east and birdsong swelled in the trees. The distant rumble of war was relentless, but it seemed nothing could daunt the birds from singing in the dawn with passion.

'How long until you can make a gateway?' Elian asked.

'A couple of minutes,' Aurora replied.

'Let's go then,' Elian ordered.

Aurora surged into a run and the thrill of launching into the sky warmed Elian's stomach as he leaned forwards, gripping the pommel of the saddle with all his strength. The great *whoosh* of Ra's first wingbeat was echoed by Shadow's just behind them. Seconds later they were airborne and climbing. They flew westwards, away from the woods, before turning back east towards the rising sun.

Elian felt Ra's inner power wax as the sun's first

rays burst forth from the horizon like a fiery diamond. Shadow raced past them as the swirling grey of the gateway formed in the sky ahead. A last glance down at the ground and Elian could just make out the woods where they had spent the night. The tiny figure he knew to be Jack was now standing in the open field to watch them go. It felt good finally to have met the man he had seen on so many of his previous visits to this world. Would Jack solve the Oracle's riddles? Elian hoped so, but further thought on the matter would have to wait. The immediacy of the yawning mouth of the vortex demanded his attention. Bracing against the horrible twisting sensation he knew was coming, he shut his eyes tight and counted slowly until he felt the gateway swallow him.

The transit through the gateway into Areth left him as disoriented as always. The sky overhead was a dark blue, lightening ahead towards the horizon. Elian judged it to be less than an hour to sunrise here in the mountains of central Orupee. They were much closer to the Oracle's cave this time – barely a minute's flying time to the ledge in front of the mouth.

The wind was light and the little bit of cloud in the sky was high above the mountaintops. The approach and landing were by far the easiest that

Elian had experienced here so far. He felt strangely wary as he dismounted, with a nagging feeling that something bad was bound to happen to compensate for the ease of their arrival.

'Hold up, Pell!' he called after his companion. 'Wait for me!'

The older boy had dismounted and was disappearing into the cave, saddlebag slung over his shoulder, striding ahead with an air of grim purpose. Elian ran, closing down the gap until he dropped into a walk alongside Pell. He looked around nervously. The guardians stepped out of their alcoves, but retreated again immediately when they recognised the two boys approaching.

'Are you all right?' Elian asked Pell in a low voice once they had moved out of the guardians' earshot.

'No,' Pell replied bluntly. 'I doubt I'm ever going to be all right again. My shoulder burns with the pain of Shadow's wound, I've been exiled from my enclave and the dark orb has used me to help kill dozens of defenceless men and animals. The Oracle has a lot to answer for, Elian. I intend to see it pay.'

'Pay? How do you intend to make the Oracle pay, Pell?'

A cold chill ran up Elian's spine. Was this what he had sensed when they landed? He looked across at Pell. The older boy appeared more determined than Elian had ever seen him before.

'You'll see soon enough,' Pell stated.

'Don't do anything foolish, Pell,' Elian pleaded. 'Let's just get rid of the orb and get out of here. The girls need our help. Segun may well have captured them. Kira and Nolita came for you when you were in trouble. Aren't you going to return that favour?'

'Segun won't waste time capturing them,' Pell replied, his voice flat and emotionless. 'If he has caught up with them, they are dead already. Segun is set on seeing the quest fail. We stand in his way. There are no boundaries he will not cross to achieve his goal. But every way you look at this, it all comes back to one thing – the Oracle. This entire mess is the Oracle's fault. It's time it stopped.'

'Stopped? How? You can't stop this, Pell.'

'Just you watch me!'

'Ra?'

'I heard,' she replied. 'Shadow can't get through to him. She tells me this is what has been distressing her so much. He is shielding his intention from her. She says his mind is a maelstrom of emotion. His surface thought patterns appear chaotic, but there is an underlying purpose that she cannot quite see through to. Stay close to him, Elian. Try to stop him from doing anything he might regret.'

'I'll *do my best,*' he promised.

No sooner had he said the words than he began to question exactly what he could do. Pell was bigger and stronger than Elian. He was also stubborn and unlikely to listen to reason. All Elian could do for now was to watch and hope.

They descended along the zigzagging ramp into the heart of the Oracle's great cavern. The light in the chamber was dim, but they had no problems seeing where they were going. Torches burned in brackets on the walls of the cavern, giving off an orange glow that forced the shadows to retreat. Elian looked at the great stalactites and stalagmites with their twisted icicle-like shapes. Was it his imagination, or had some of them changed position since he was last here? He dismissed the idea instantly as ludicrous. There was no way a cave formed from solid rock could change shape in a matter of days.

As they approached it, the circular opening in the chamber floor gaped black and lifeless. The low wall that encircled the great hole seemed like the rim of a huge sunken cup, filled to the brim with the very substance of night. The darkness inside was so dense it looked solid.

A distant whisper breathed through the air as Elian and Pell approached the heart of the chamber.

The Oracle was coming. Elian's muscles tightened with nervousness. He looked around to check that Aurora was close. She was right behind him, with Shadow moving alongside her. Twisting tendrils of mist began to rise from the dark well. They twirled and danced, teasing the boys' eyes with hints of recognisable shapes before morphing and evolving into something different and equally tantalising.

The suddenness of the Oracle's arrival was as breathtaking as ever. One moment the smoke-like pillar of mist was insubstantial and formless, the next it glared at them with the burning eyes of a great dragon's head.

'*I sense ye return triumphant, Master Pell.*' The Oracle's voice echoed around the chamber with a resonance that made the very air seem alive. Somehow it also rang within their minds, leaving Elian unsure if it had really spoken or not. '*Thou hast the Orb of Death. Yet all is not well. I feel it in your mind.*'

'You're damned right all is not well!' Pell shouted, his face dark with rage. 'You expected me to return here bearing my dragon's heart wrapped in crystal. I was imprisoned, exiled and tested to the limits to win my own dragon's death without my knowing it. Even then it didn't end. You knew full well that this monstrosity of a globe would kill at every sunset. The Creator only knows how many it would have killed if Elian and Aurora had not taken us through that hellish other world and brought us here quickly. What sort of sick and twisted creature are you to make such an evil creation?'

Elian watched with his heart beating fast as Pell reached into his saddlebag and drew out a ball of cloth. With delicate care, Shadow's rider peeled back the layers until the dark orb sat in a cradle of cloth atop his cupped hand.

'*Ahhh!*' the Oracle sighed on seeing the orb. The light in the room brightened slightly. '*Come. Toss the orb into my well. Be rid of it, Pell. To bear it for too long will send a man insane. You have done well to bring it so far still retaining your senses.*'

Was that a note of avarice in the Oracle's voice? Why was it ignoring Pell's questions? Where on previous encounters he had felt awestruck by the spirit creature's presence, suddenly Elian felt uncertainty and a twinge of fear. Pell had made valid points. Why should the Oracle's rebirth require others to die? Was it really the wholesome creature the dragons believed it to be? Had it been deceiving and manipulating them across generations of dragons? Elian poured his thoughts through the bond to Aurora. She made no response, but he could feel her doubts growing, too.

149

'No,' Pell said, raising the orb high above his head. 'I'm not giving you the orb. It ends here and now. Unless you give me the answers I want, I'll smash it.'

Elian instinctively drew in a deep breath and held it. His eyes flicked back and forth between the Oracle and the orb as he waited for the spirit creature to respond to the challenge. He expected the Oracle to be angered by Pell's belligerence, but once again he was surprised. It sighed, a long whispering sigh that conveyed disappointment and deep hurt. The burning eyes dimmed and for long moments it was silent.

'The orbs are not my creation,' it admitted slowly, sounding old and tired. *'The truth is I do not fully understand them. The plinths were made by an ancient race, long dead now. The secrets of the orbs and how they were formed, died with them. I make no excuses for the orbs, or what they do. I like their properties no more than you do. If I were not the last of my kind, I would gladly move on to the next realm without invoking their power. But if I die now, Areth will be plunged into anarchy – and I have worked too hard for too long to let that happen. I refuse to leave Areth to the mercy of the night dragon enclave. The day dragons, for all their bravery, cannot hope to contain the night dragons' lust for power. Whilst I remain, dragonkind is bound to*

my purpose. I must survive, Pell. Segun and the others must be held in check. The fate of all Areth depends on it.'

Chapter Thirteen
The Grand Library

'The place where the shadows dwell,' Kalen repeated thoughtfully. 'That sounds familiar. Something tells me I've heard the phrase before ... but where?'

'There's a rhyme that relates to it,' Kira said. 'It was all we were given in order to complete this part of our quest. It goes like this:

> *'Ever protected, the dusk orb lies*
> *Behind the cover, yet no disguise.*
> *Afterlife image, unreal yet real,*
> *Lives in the shadows, waits to reveal.*

'Does that help?'

Kalen's forehead scrunched into deep furrows. Kira and Nolita waited, barely able to breathe. Then the old man shook his head slowly and Kira could taste the bitterness of disappointment.

'No,' he said. 'That doesn't help at all. I thought for a moment that it might be the name of a painting. There are several artists whose works focus on shadow and light. It may be that I'm thinking of a picture I've seen entitled "Place of Shadows", or something similar. The rhyme gives a different edge to the meaning, though. Of course, it's possible that I'm thinking along the right track. A painting is an image. It could be a picture of an imagined afterlife that has been hung somewhere in the shadows. That's probably wishful thinking, though. Hmm. Where could we learn more about a place where shadows dwell?'

'I thought that "afterlife image" might refer to a ghost,' Nolita offered. 'Or something that looks like a ghost.'

Kalen looked at her through narrowed eyes and crossed his arms.

'You look far too sensible a girl to believe in such things,' he said. 'People like to write stories about such nonsense to scare and thrill. What little study time I wasted on so-called ghostly apparitions has convinced me they are nothing but superstitious nonsense. No, it's the clause "unreal, yet real" that gives us the best clue. It could be that it refers to someone who pretends to be a ghost.'

'But the Oracle is a spirit creature,' Kira protested.

'The Oracle? I've heard that dragons talk of an Oracle. I thought it was one of their own kind – an ancient dragon that gives out quests to riders. A sort of high leader.'

'No,' Nolita answered, her voice firm and confident. 'We've encountered it twice now. It's difficult to describe the Oracle. It's alive, yet it appears insubstantial – almost as if it's made of smoke. It lives in a cave in the mountains of Central Orupee and is highly revered by the dragons. It sent us on this quest. The Oracle is inspiring, scary and very real.'

'Really?' Kalen said, his eyebrows rising. He did not look convinced. 'I've seen illusions created from smoke. They can be most convincing. But I hesitate to doubt the word of a dragonrider, so I will not rule anything out. Come. Let's go and look in the general reference section and see where our research takes us.'

The old scholar set out towards the interlocking maze of immense bookcases ahead of them. He weaved through the towering corridors of books with supreme confidence. Kira was glad of his guidance. To her untutored eye all the bookcases looked the same. It seemed worse than navigating a jungle.

Looking up at the soaring dome above them, Kira realised they were approaching the very centre of the enormous circular chamber. Distracted by the amazing decoration on the huge dome roof high above, she did not notice when Kalen stopped, and she accidentally bumped into him. Nolita was also caught by surprise, but managed to sidestep the scholar at the last moment.

'Sorry!' Kira apologised, taking a step backwards.

'Think nothing of it,' he mumbled, already studying the books on the shelf at chest height. He ran his right index finger across the books, his head to one side as he studied the words and symbols. He ducked down and did the same on the shelf below until his finger came to rest on a thick black leather-bound volume with silvery writing across the spine. 'Ah! Here we are,' he said, tipping the top of the book forwards before grasping it more firmly and drawing it out from between its neighbours. 'Let's take a look in here. Come. There's a study area just around the corner.'

He set off with a sense of purpose in his stride. Kira and Nolita glanced at one another and shrugged at precisely the same moment. Kira's lips twitched into a smile. She found the library intimidating and felt out of her depth, but Nolita's simultaneous reaction to the scholar's enthusiasm for the books made her relax.

'Can you read?' she whispered.

Nolita looked at her with surprise. 'No. I assumed you could.'

'I'm a hunter. What would I know about reading books?'

Their smiles broadened as the irony of their situation sank in. Here they were, surrounded by the largest collection of information in the known world, and neither of them could read a word. They moved to follow the old scholar.

'Let's hope Kalen knows what he's doing,' Nolita whispered.

At the end of the next bookcase was an open area with half a dozen large tables surrounded by upright wooden chairs. Several scholars sat at the table with books and scrolls spread across the surface. One or two of them glanced up at the new arrivals, but quickly settled their attention back to their work. Kalen seated himself at an empty table, opened the cover of the big black book and began thumbing through the pages.

Kira and Nolita sat either side of him. The lines of curious symbols on the creamy yellow pages meant nothing to them, but they held the girls' attention as Kalen flicked through page after page of them. Occasionally there were beautiful line illustrations, which Kira found particularly interesting.

As the minutes slid by, the unintelligible text lost its allure and Kira found her mind wandering. She looked up and discovered that Nolita was also restless, looking around the Grand Library for something to pass the time.

The silence in the huge chamber thickened. Kira gave an involuntary shiver. It felt almost as though a malevolent spirit inhabited the library, lurking amongst the labyrinth of bookcases. The atmosphere was close and oppressive, as if a thunderstorm were about to unleash its fury within the enormous arching dome above. Her hunter's sense was tingling and her eyes scanned the surrounding bookcases with growing nervousness.

'Pah!' Kalen said suddenly, startling both Kira and Nolita and instantly dispelling the growing sense of impending disaster. He gave a snort of disgust and snapped the heavy book shut with a thump. 'Nothing! We'll have to look elsewhere.'

'Um . . . Kalen?' Kira began in a soft voice.

'Yes?' he replied absently. His brow furrowed as his mind concentrated on where to look next.

'Is there anywhere that Nolita and I might be able to get something to eat and drink?'

'In the Grand Library!' Kalen said, looking shocked. 'Most certainly not! The books here are priceless. Food and drink are never allowed inside for fear of the damage they might cause.'

'I don't want to offend, sir, but would you mind if we left you to the search for a short while?' she asked. 'We're hungry and thirsty after our long flight. It probably doesn't help that we can't read.'

'Can't read!' he exclaimed. 'Good heavens! How can you live without being able to read?' He paused for a moment, but from his expression it was clear that the question was rhetorical. 'Go back through the main doors and turn to your left. About halfway along the colonnade you will find a door that leads into a street filled with vendors of food and drink. I assume you have money enough to buy food?'

'I don't have any local currency, but I do have some silver and copper coins from my home country. Will these be acceptable, do you think?'

Kira pulled out some coins from her belt pouch and held them out to Kalen. He picked up a silver coin and turned it over in his fingers, inspecting it minutely. After a moment he gave the coin back and nodded.

'They should be fine,' he said, 'but the vendors will make you pay over the going price if you use those. Exchange some money before you buy anything. The moneylenders should give you a rate of one to one at worst. Don't accept anything less. Your silvers are slightly larger and heavier than the local ones. Whenever you buy anything – even exchanging coins – be sure to haggle. Everyone haggles here. It's expected.'

'Thank you,' Kira replied. 'But I feel guilty leaving you to search out answers for us.'

'Not at all,' Kalen said, a broad smile across his face. 'I can assure you it's my pleasure. We scholars live to find answers. It's what makes us feel most alive.'

'One last thing,' Kira said tentatively.

'Yes?'

'How do we find our way through the maze of bookshelves to the front doors?'

'A good question,' he answered. He pointed up at the ceiling of the dome. 'Do you see the dark blue line that runs across the diameter of the dome? That's a meridian line. It runs from the front of the building to the back. The front end has a gold band. At the rear there's a silver band. Just keep turning towards the end of the blue line with the gold band and you won't go wrong. There are many ways in and out of the bookshelves. It isn't difficult.'

'Thank you again. We'll try not to be too long.'

'Don't worry,' Kalen said, waving them ahead. 'There's no rush. I've got a feeling it's going to take me a while to find the reference we're looking for.'

Kalen walked behind them until they reached the shelf where the large black book was housed. He replaced the book and instantly began to search for another volume. The two girls continued, turning to follow the meridian line as the scholar had instructed.

As they weaved through the tall bookcases, Kira's hunter's instinct began to tingle again. Her body prickled and tensed, much as it had before the ice worms attacked. Was something stalking her here in the library? If so, what? The very notion was ridiculous. What manner of creature would hunt in a library?

'Are you all right, Kira?' Nolita whispered in a low voice. 'You keep looking around. Is something wrong?'

'I don't know,' she replied, leaning close and speaking softly. 'But stay alert. My instincts are telling me trouble is not far away.'

'Is it Kalen?'

'No,' Kira said quickly. 'At least I don't think so. But I'll feel a lot more comfortable when we're out in the open air.'

They reached the edge of the maze and the girls

picked up their pace as they crossed the open floor to the main doors. Kira let out a long, silent sigh of relief as they stepped into the bright sunlight. The air outside was not pleasant, but the sense of impending disaster lifted and she began to relax. They turned left and descended the great marble steps in a diagonal line towards the colonnade to the left of the enormous courtyard.

Kira glanced back at the main doors and shrugged. I'm getting paranoid, she thought, pursing her lips into a thin line. I must be.

'The place where shadows *dwell* . . . the place where *shadows* dwell . . . the place *where* shadows dwell . . .' Kalen repeated the phrase softly over and over again as his eyes skimmed the bookshelves looking for inspiration. He changed the emphasis each time to try to trigger something – anything in his memory that might give him a clue as to where he had heard the phrase before.

'What could such a place be?' he muttered. 'Could it be a puppet theatre? Puppets are figurative shadows of the people they are meant to represent. Or even a theatre of shadows?' His mind leapt back to his own crude efforts to form representations of birds, dogs and other animals by creating shadow figures with his hands. There were those who performed amazing shows using only shadows. Could that be the meaning of the words? Was he looking for some sort of theatre house? Why then would the accompanying verse talk of an afterlife image? Puppets were not ghosts. But what if a puppet theatre existed that only featured puppets that looked like ghosts? It was a ludicrous idea! He was trying to twist the words to fit his theory.

'That's not the path of a true scholar, Kalen,' he told himself sternly. 'Think!'

Were the girls right? Could he be looking for somewhere haunted? Where in the library would he find information about purportedly haunted places? It was not something he had ever taken seriously, but he knew there were those for whom ghostly encounters were a most serious subject matter. There had to be a section devoted to such things, but where?

'The master index,' he muttered. 'I suppose it's the obvious place to go.'

It was humiliating to have to resort to the library's index system. He had spent years in this library and knew certain sections of it so well he could recite the titles of the books in sequence across the shelves without looking. The index book was kept on its own table not far from where he had been sitting with the two dragonriders.

He re-entered the central study area and strode between the tables with a gait that spoke of both purpose and a touch of anger.

'Ah, Kalen, my good friend!'

Kalen stopped as if he had walked into a stone wall. The voice was unmistakeable. He turned and bowed deeply, careful not to make eye contact until he had completed his bow.

'High Lord Tarpone,' he said, trying to sound pleased. 'To what do I owe the pleasure? We don't see you here in the library very often these days.'

Kalen lifted his head from his instinctive bow and saw that the High Lord was not alone. Next to him stood a tall man dressed in black. He had dark hair and piercing eyes of the palest blue, set deep under heavy brows. The man wore a smile that was as cold as the ice in his gaze. There was an aura of power about him far stronger than that of the High Lord. His posture screamed strength and authority.

'No, my old friend,' Tarpone said gravely. 'My duties keep me absent from my studies all too often these days. Alas, this visit is also not for my own benefit. I'd like to introduce you to an old friend of mine. Kalen, this is Lord Segun, leader of the night dragon enclave.'

Chapter Fourteen
'Not Again!'

'Pell! Don't!' Elian yelled instinctively, his panic rising as he thought of what might happen if the orb were smashed. He took a step towards the older boy, his hands palm forwards in an unmistakeable signal for Pell to stop. 'We've come too far. Do you want all that pain to count for nothing? Don't be a fool. You've made your point. Now give the orb to the Oracle and let's get out of here.'

'No, Elian,' Pell replied, his voice laced with ice. 'The Oracle hasn't been honest with us from the start. It's time that changed.' He faced the towering smoke creature and met its burning gaze. 'Tell us the location of the dusk orb,' he ordered. 'In plain language.'

'*That is not permitted.*' The Oracle's denial echoed around the chamber, the rumbling repetitions emphasising the statement. Elian's heart raced as the creature's eyes burned with anger. Was Pell crazy? How could he stand to look into those burning eyes without feeling fear? As far as Elian could see, the only emotion in Pell's eyes was defiance.

'Not permitted by whom?' Pell asked. 'It seems to me that *you* make the rules for this game. Change the rules. Tell us where the dusk orb is.'

The Oracle fell silent. Its gaze never left the orb in Pell's raised hands. The silence brewed, seeming to thicken with intensity as Elian tried to count his rapid heartbeats.

'*I do not make the rules, Pell,*' it said suddenly. '*And even if I were to reveal the location, thou wouldst gain nothing from the knowledge. It is not thy place to retrieve the third orb. Only Kira and Longfang may complete this phase of the quest.*'

'If we do not benefit from your telling us, then you have no reason not to do it,' Pell reasoned, raising the orb of death still higher.

The Oracle considered again for a moment. '*This is true,*' it conceded. '*Thou hast been separated from those whose task it is to find the third orb. They cannot gain from the knowledge unless thou canst find them. Very well. It is not the normal way, but I will do it this once. Throw the orb into my well and I will reveal the location of the next.*'

Elian was astonished. Pell had done it. He had backed the Oracle into a corner and won. Why then was he hesitating? Elian could see him wavering, indecision clear on his face. 'Do it!' he urged through gritted teeth.

'I'm no longer sure we can trust the Oracle,' Pell said, shifting his focus briefly to glance at Elian. 'None of our dealings with it so far have been straightforward. Why should I trust it to keep its word? Once it has the orb we have nothing left to bargain with. I don't know which I dislike more – this twisted creature with its riddles, its ulterior motives and its deceptions, or Segun. At least Segun is open with his intentions, even if his heart is as black as the devil's armpit.'

The enormous dragon's head leaned forwards on its vaporous neck until its nostrils were no more than a couple of fingers' widths in front of Pell. Its eyes burned bright with red anger.

'*Thou treadst on dangerous ground, youngling. Do not test my patience any further. Give me the orb, or destroy it and watch thy future die with me. I have said I will reveal where the third orb awaits. Think what thou wilt, I do not lie.*'

With a suddenness that was shocking, Pell brought his arms downwards as if to hurl the orb at the rock in front of his feet. Elian sucked in a sharp intake of breath that hissed through his teeth and he felt the two dragons behind him surge forwards in an instinctive effort to prevent the orb from being smashed. Had Pell let go of the orb, neither would have reached it in time. But he did not. Instead he hung onto the black crystal globe and rather than smashing it, he reversed the momentum and tossed it upwards in a gentle arc that carried it over the low wall in front of him to drop into the bottomless blackness that was the Oracle's pit.

For a moment Elian's knees wobbled as he fought to stay upright. His stomach felt as if it had climbed his throat and his heart was hammering so hard that he thought it might bruise itself on his ribs.

'Ahh!' the Oracle breathed, its smoky form shifting and then solidifying again. '*Thank you. The second orb brings a bittersweet flavour. It will take time for me to absorb its energy. I must rest.*'

'The location you promised?' Pell persisted, anger punching out the key syllables.

'*The Castle of Shadows.*' The answer came in a whisper, as the towering form collapsed inwards on itself. '*Seek the Castle of Shadows.*'

The last wisp of smoke sucked down into the darkness, leaving the vast chamber dim and echoing with the final flowing rush of the Oracle's departure. Elian turned and staggered across to Aurora. He leaned against her foreleg, his entire body shaking with the aftershock of emotion he felt from the encounter. The Castle of Shadows? he thought, his mind sounding out the name carefully. Even its title bears an uncomfortable chill.

'*It is a dark place,*' Aurora confirmed. '*Dragons do not go there any more.*'

'*Really? Why not?*' Elian asked.

Aurora did not reply. This was not like her at all. The bond between their minds turned cold, as if a chill wind were blowing across the link. He pushed away from her leg and looked her in the eye.

'*What is it, Ra? Why don't dragons go there?*' he persisted.

Still she hesitated to respond. When finally she did, her voice resonated in his skull, slow and serious.

'*Because those who enter its gates never return,*' she said.

'Hell and damnation!' Jack swore, fighting the controls as the aircraft lost power and nosed down into a dive. 'Not again!'

A thick plume of smoke erupted from his engine, coiled around the fuselage and trailed across the sky behind him like a gigantic black serpent. Hot oil ran in long black streaks from just aft of the propellor.

Unless he landed quickly he was likely to be toasted. A fire in the engine would quickly spread through the wood and fabric. He had no parachute, so his only option was to crash land and get away from the wreckage as quickly as he could.

To crash once and walk away was fortunate. A second time in less than a week would require little short of a miracle.

It was his own fault to think he could take on the Red Baron, but he had been hot-headed with thoughts of vengeance. The top German flying ace, Baron Manfred Von Richthofen, nicknamed the Red Baron for his distinctive red tri-plane, together with his infamous 'flying circus' of talented pilots, had attacked from above. Jack had spotted them coming, but despite all his efforts to warn his wingman by waggling his wings and pitching his air-craft up and down, the junior pilot had appeared unaware of the approaching danger.

Von Richthofen and his men had been almost on top of them before Jack's sense of self-preservation forced him to turn away from his wingman and take the fight to the enemy. The poor lad, fresh out of flying training, had stood no chance. Jack only hoped the boy had not suffered as he went down.

It was foolish to go after the German ace, but Jack's anger had made him rash. Despite the sky being full of enemy machines, he had been in no mood to run. To his surprise, however, he had only managed to get off a couple of ineffectual bursts in the general direction of the red tri-plane before the fight had turned against him.

Von Richthofen was good – really good. His machine twisted and turned so fast that it seemed almost to disappear and reappear on Jack's tail. Having traded places from hunter to hunted in less than a minute, Jack was horrified as a line of bullets ripped through his machine and his engine began to cough and splutter. Vibrations rippled through the cockpit. They were intermittent to begin, but soon built in a crescendo that rattled his teeth and sent an icy finger of fear pressing deep into his stomach.

Jack did not see the arrival of the flight of allied aircraft. All his attention was on staying alive and trying to keep his ailing aircraft in the air. Had it not been for the newcomers entering the fray, Von Richthofen would most likely have pursued him further and made sure of his kill. Instead, the Baron's bright red Fokker tri-plane raced past him, sights set on a new target. Jack's emotions were a strange mix. He felt insignificant, yet lucky at the same time.

Everywhere he looked now, aircraft turned,

dived and spat death at one another. It was one of the most intense dogfights he had ever seen.

'Unbelievable!' he thought. 'One minute I have the Red Baron in my sights, the next he shoots me down!'

The sight of that red machine peeling away and latching onto the tail of another Allied aircraft ignited the blood in his veins still further. Anger burned, reinforcing his determination to survive. He should have known better than to hang around when he saw that large formation: Von Richthofen always patrolled with a large wing of talented pilots around him. And now Jack knew the deal he would propose to the dragonriders – if he could just live long enough to make the offer. The dragons did not want to commit to joining the war effort – fine. One mission would be enough.

Manfred Von Richthofen had been a menace to Allied forces since long before Jack had joined his first squadron. Amongst the flying aces of the enemy, he held the reputation for being the deadliest. What a blow it would be to the enemy's morale if he could be killed, or better still – captured. The German Luftwaffe had dominated the air above the trenches for months. The loss of no single man would turn the tide of the air war overnight. Jack was enough of a realist to see that.

Immelmann, Boelke, Hawker, Ball ... all had seemed like gods of the air in their day, yet one by one they had fallen victim to chance, arrogance or a superior opponent. Von Richthofen had outlived them all – and still his tally mounted.

It was rumoured that Von Richthofen had a silver goblet made to commemorate each aircraft he shot down. The idea that Jack's crash would give the German pilot cause to commission another trophy today made him all the more determined to survive. The trick would be to keep the airspeed under control.

'Concentrate,' he muttered. 'Don't let it get away from you.'

The engine was no longer producing any power. He peered at the altimeter. It showed two-and-a-half thousand feet remaining. His airspeed was much too high and he was descending too fast. Smoke poured from the front of the aircraft, swirling around the cockpit and making it difficult to see. The oily smoke set Jack coughing. The taste of it was foul, but even with his stomach heaving and his chest in spasm he did not panic. With cool discipline he fought the controls, dragging the machine out of its steep spiral descent and into a controllable shallow dive.

As the airspeed reduced, so the cloud of smoke

around Jack intensified. He couldn't see anything. Droplets of hot oil were spattering across his goggles. Landing blind was impossible. He had to stop the smoke from flowing directly back over the cockpit. The only way he knew to change the airflow drastically was to put the aircraft into a severe sideslip. He wasted no time. Forcing the yolk to the left, he dipped the left wing whilst simultaneously kicking the rudder pedal to the right in opposition to the turn.

With the controls deliberately held in opposite directions the aircraft began sliding sideways at the ground. The rate of descent increased until it seemed the aircraft was almost falling vertically out of the sky, but it had the desired effect. The smoke stream from the engine detached from the fuselage and poured over the right wing.

The ground was approaching rapidly, the aircraft slicing towards the earth at a lethal rate of descent. Although the air now flowing through the cockpit was clear, Jack hardly dared to breathe. The final few seconds required perfect anticipation, or he would smash into the ground with such force that there would be no chance of his walking away.

An open field loomed ahead. It was far from flat, which was not ideal for a forced landing, but he had no choice. The airspeed was fluctuating wildly on the gauge, but this was not unusual when side-slipping. The approach felt all wrong – the steep descent, the unstable airspeed, the fact that he was looking out of the front left side of the cockpit rather than over the nose – everything. At the last possible moment he straightened the aircraft into normal flight and attempted to check the rate of descent. His anticipation was almost perfect – *almost*.

The moment of impact was horrific. He had judged his final flare to perfection, but the aeroplane was not quite straight as it touched down. There was an almighty crack as the right main undercarriage leg sheared away. The right wing caught the ground and for a moment the world appeared to spin and whirl in a totally incomprehensible fashion. Jack was flung from one side of the cockpit to the other, bruising both shoulders, but amazingly sustaining no other injuries.

What was left of the aircraft came to a stop. For the briefest moment, Jack sat motionless, unable to believe he was still alive. A huge sheet of bright orange flame erupted from the engine in front of him. A moment later Jack was looking back at the wreckage from about fifty yards up the gentle slope. How he had got there was a blank spot in his memory. He could only assume that his survival instinct and a rush of adrenalin had ruled his brain for the intervening time.

The cockpit was engulfed in flame. The right wing had been totally torn off during the crash landing. The tattered remainder of it was some seventy yards back from the rest of the wreckage, probably the only piece of the aircraft to remain once the fire had burned itself out. Jack sank down suddenly into the deep grass, as his legs seemed to turn to jelly. A wave of relief left him weak and shaking uncontrollably. He glanced instinctively at the sky where the fight was still raging. Two further aircraft trailed black smoke: one in a dive from which there would be no lucky escape, the other still manoeuvring hard. From this range he could not tell if they were friendly, or not.

Looking back at the flames leaping from the wreckage that had been his aeroplane just moments before, it seemed impossible that he had survived. 'How in God's holy name did I get away with that?' he breathed.

The engine chose that moment to explode and Jack fell back flat into the grass. Instinct made him wrap his arms across his face. It was only then that he noticed he was clutching something in his right hand. It was his map. On the back of it were written the words of the Oracle's rhyming verses. He did not remember grabbing it from the cockpit, but then he did not remember much of the last few minutes at all. He was glad to have the written copy of the verses. Solving the riddles without that would have been impossible.

'If I didn't know better, I'd be tempted to believe someone was looking after me today,' he muttered. His lips twisted into a wry smile and his eyes flicked heavenward. 'If you are, then thanks,' he added.

Jack had hardly set foot inside a church in his life, but at this moment he felt obliged to thank someone for keeping him alive. Even if no one was listening, it made him feel good.

He sat up and checked the map to see if the words he had written on the back of it were still legible. They were. He smiled. It was a wonderful moment. Walking away from the burning wreckage of his aircraft made him feel he was beginning another life – gifted with a chance to start again.

'Start again . . .' he muttered. 'That's it!'

He lifted the map and scanned through the poem. The answers were obvious. Why had he not seen them before? He knew the answers – all of them. He had what the dragonriders needed. They had what he needed. With their help he could take his revenge on Von Richthofen and strike a devastating blow for the Allies. But he had no way to contact them. The irony of it was priceless.

Jack threw his head back and laughed. It was all he could do.

Chapter Fifteen
Murder

Kalen felt deeply troubled as he watched the High Lord and his dragonrider friend, Segun, leave. Tarpone had never been a true scholar. He had dabbled with study on and off for many years, but had never taken it seriously. Even as a youth, the man who had risen to become High Lord had always been far more interested in money and status. He had been born to a wealthy family, and had used his father's influence and fortune to achieve ultimate power in Harkesis.

'What are you up to, Tarpone?' Kalen muttered under his breath. 'Do you know what you're doing? Segun is attempting to sabotage the quest of the two young girls. He's a nasty piece of work, or I'm no scholar. Why help him? Feeding Kira and Nolita misinformation will serve no good purpose.'

Stroking his chin thoughtfully, Kalen tried to dismiss the visit from his mind. He knew to tread carefully around the High Lord. Even though he had maintained a relationship that bordered on friendship with Tarpone for many years, he knew their long association would count for nothing if he did not do as he had been asked.

'Find the answer to the riddle first,' he told himself. 'You can worry about what to do with it once you've figured out the answer.'

He went to the master index and began thumbing through it until he found the reference he wanted. The books he needed were in the North Hall.

'I should have known!' he grumbled, closing the master index.

The North Hall was several degrees cooler than the rest of the Grand Library and Kalen had developed a particular distaste for it during the past few years. His old bones increasingly felt the cold and he avoided working there as a matter of habit.

He looked around at the men studying at the tables nearby. They were immersed in their work, but there was one he felt he could trust to relate a message.

'Conrad?' he asked, speaking boldly to attract the man's attention. 'Conrad, would you mind doing me a small service?'

'That depends, Kalen,' the scholar replied. 'I'm rather busy at the moment.'

'I need someone to pass on a message. Are you going to be here for a while longer?' Kalen asked.

'Yes, I'll be here all day.'

'Good. Did you notice the two young female dragonriders I was with earlier?'

'I did.'

'They have gone to get something to eat,' Kalen explained. 'They'll not be long. Could you tell them I've gone to the North Hall, please? I'm seeking the answer to a riddle for them. Rather than risk their getting lost, could you ask them to wait for me here?'

'Of course, Kalen,' the old man replied. 'I shall watch for them.'

Kalen thanked Conrad and set off through the maze of bookcases. The riddle was all the more tantalising now. With at least two distinct factions of dragonriders involved in the search, he knew the answer was important. Dragonriders did not chase shadows without reason – especially not someone like Segun. Something big was happening. Maybe if he found the answer to the riddle, he would be considered worthy of being elevated to the gold sash.

The most prestigious level of scholarship had

eluded Kalen for decades. It had been over twenty season rotations since he had been raised to the purple sash for his book on social dynamics. To be awarded purple was a great honour and Kalen was proud of his achievements, but the dream of every scholar was to achieve the ultimate accolade. There were only three living scholars in all Harkesis who wore the gold. Perhaps this was his chance to join that most elite group of scholars. To solve a riddle that eluded the minds of dragons – surely that would be considered special. But if it proved easy, would it be special enough? Perhaps he should drag out his findings – make the discovery more dramatic.

His pace quickened as his excitement mounted. By the time he reached the North Hall he was marching between the bookcases with a stride that spoke of urgency and purpose. His focus was fixed and his mind was racing through possibilities. Given his preoccupation, it was perhaps not surprising that he did not notice the silent figure following his every move.

'Kalen has gone to the North Hall to seek an answer to your riddle.'

Kira smiled at the old scholar. 'Thank you, sir,' she replied. 'I did wonder how we were going to

181

find him in this huge library. Could you direct us to the North Hall, please? We're not familiar with the layout.'

'He asked me to tell you to remain here until he returns,' the man replied. 'If you go looking for him, you might miss one another and circle endlessly.'

'You're quite right, sir,' Kira said, her heart sinking at the thought of having to sit here and wait for Kalen to return. 'Has he been gone long?'

'Oh, some time now, I think,' Conrad replied, looking down at his book and trying to remember. 'Judging by how much I've read since I spoke to him, I'd say it must be more than an hour since he left. Kalen is a most competent scholar. If your answer can be found, then he will find it.'

Kira did not ask what would happen if the answer could not be found. She thanked him again and drew Nolita across to an unoccupied table. Lunch had been an experience she would not forget in a hurry. Life in the city was very different from life in the savannah and jungle of southern Racafi. She could tell that Nolita felt as uncomfortable as she did. The prickle of her hunter's instinct had begun again the moment they stepped through the great doors of the Grand Library. With her nerves on edge and her eyes constantly scanning for signs of danger, Kira slowly sat down.

Her bottom barely touched the chair before she was on her feet again. A shout reverberated through the air shaking her to the core.

'MURDER! MURDER IN THE LIBRARY!'

It was hard to tell where the shout had come from, but Kira caught the eye of the old scholar and he pointed without hesitation. She was in motion in a heartbeat. A glance up at the meridian line on the great dome gave her the reference she needed. Her hunting knife was in her hand, though she did not remember drawing it. Nolita ran alongside her. The blonde girl also held a gleaming blade at the ready. Kira had felt the menace in the air from the moment she arrived. She was not going to be caught unprepared if they came face to face with the source of the dark aura.

Weaving between the bookcases at speed, they quickly emerged from the maze. The moment she saw the body on the floor in the doorway, Kira knew it was Kalen. Four younger men in white robes surrounded him. Kira accelerated into a sprint.

'Get away from him!' she warned as she skidded to a stop on the mosaic tiled floor. 'All of you – get away from him. Now!'

One look at Kira's face was enough. The gleam of clean steel in her hand reinforced the reaction. Three of the men backed away, their hands raised in a gesture of peace. The fourth did not move. He had his right hand on Kalen's back and his left was feeling the side of the old man's neck. A large pool of blood was creeping across the floor.

'I can't feel a pulse, but the blood is still spreading,' the young scholar said, sounding both panicked and frightened. 'What should we do?'

'Get away from him,' Kira repeated. 'Let me see. Do you have medics nearby?'

'Not nearby, but we can send for them.'

'Then do it. Quickly!'

One of the young scholars turned and ran in the direction of the main entrance.

The young man kneeling by Kalen slowly got to his feet and stepped back to join his remaining colleagues. Kira was quick to take his place. She laid her blade down gently on Kalen's lower back. The back of his robe was totally soaked with blood and a trail of blood led back into the North Hall. The old man must have dragged himself some distance across the floor to the doorway.

There were two holes through the back of his robe. Whoever stabbed him knew what he was doing. Both wounds were horizontal. The killer had struck low enough to miss the tough bone of the shoulder blade, but high enough to slip the blade between the ribs and into Kalen's lungs. It was no wonder that the old scholar had not cried out when he was attacked.

As Kira made her assessment of the wounds another young scholar came running across the North Hall waving a piece of parchment.

'I found this,' he gasped.

Kira ignored him, maintaining her focus on Kalen.

'What is it, Mikhal?' asked the young scholar who had been last to move away from Kalen.

'It was on the floor next to the place where the blood trail begins,' Mikhal panted. 'It just has a single word on it: "Darkenfell". Do you think it's important?'

Nolita gasped and Kira glanced at her. The blonde girl's face looked pale with shock, but whether that was at the sight of Kalen's body, or at the name the young scholar had mentioned was unclear.

'What is it, Nolita?' she asked. 'Have you heard of Darkenfell? Where is it?'

'It's an evil name,' Nolita replied, her voice barely more than a whisper. 'No one goes there by choice.'

'Well we may have to,' Kira said, her voice hard as iron. 'Where is this Darkenfell? I've never heard of it before.'

'It's on the far side of Northern Cemaria.'

'Damn!' Kira swore, her hands clenching tight into fists. 'It would be! It'll take us weeks to get there without Elian and Aurora. Weeks we don't have.'

'Let me see that piece of paper, Mikhal,' said a deep voice from behind them.

It was Conrad, the old scholar who had directed them from the central study area of the library. A small crowd had gathered from all directions, but it was Conrad who stepped forwards. The young man held the piece of parchment out to his senior. He assessed it with a single glance and waved it away.

'Strange,' he said thoughtfully. 'That's not Kalen's handwriting.'

To Kira's complete surprise, Kalen's body and right arm began to move. Startled, she flinched and overbalanced, falling away from him and scrabbling quickly to regain her feet. Conrad quickly took her place, crouching down and talking to Kalen in a low, encouraging voice. 'What is it, old friend? Yes it's me, Conrad. Relax. We're here now.'

Kalen raised his right hand slightly, pinching his thumb and first two fingers together.

'A quill,' Conrad ordered. 'Someone give me a quill. You there! Take a book from the shelf behind

186

you. Any book. It doesn't matter which one.'

Someone gave Conrad a quill, which he, in turn, placed gently between Kalen's questing fingers.

'The book, man! Come on! He doesn't have long.'

'But it'll be ruined, sir!' the junior replied, a note of anguish in his voice.

'I'll take responsibility for that. Now do as you're told.'

With trembling fingers the junior handed Conrad a thin, leather-bound book. Without hesitation the old scholar opened it to the blank final page and placed the book down into the pool of blood underneath Kalen's hand. Shaking with effort, Kalen trawled the nib of the quill through the pool of blood and began scratching out a string of spidery letters on the open page. It seemed to take an age for him to form each symbol, but Conrad was nodding and muttering encouragement throughout. Tears formed in Kira's eyes as she watched the determination of the dying man to complete his message.

With a horrible gurgling groan, Kalen's whole body suddenly tensed and then relaxed into death. The word was left unfinished, a trailing line of blood dragged across the rest of the page marking his final moment of life.

Kira scanned the small crowd of scholars. They were all wearing light-coloured robes. The only person aside from Conrad and herself who had any blood on them was the young man who had knelt by Kalen's side when she had first approached. He did not have the look of a killer. The old man had dragged himself a considerable distance from where he had been attacked. The murderer would be long gone by now.

'Did he name his attacker?' she asked, looking at the strange red symbols Kalen had scratched into the book.

Conrad shook his head. 'No,' he said, sounding puzzled. 'His dying wish was to solve your riddle, but I'm not sure what his message means.'

'What does it say?' Kira asked, trying to banish any eagerness from her voice.

'It's not easy to read,' Conrad said slowly. 'But I think it says: "Not Darkenfell. Castle of Shadows. Night ..." then there is one final word that might be "drag" or "drags". He didn't finish it, so I can't be sure.'

'Could it be "dragons"?' Nolita asked.

'He could have been trying to write "dragons", but it's impossible to say for sure,' the scholar replied. 'Does the message mean anything to you?'

'I don't know,' Kira replied, eyeing the people

around cautiously. 'It might do. It appears that whoever left the scrap of parchment with "Darkenfell" written on it was looking to mislead us. Has anyone heard of a Castle of Shadows?'

Kira turned in a slow, deliberate circle. She was surrounded by pale-faced scholars whose expressions varied between shock, sadness and outrage. Was one of them a murderer? Would the killer stay to see if he had achieved his aim? Her instincts told her the killer was gone.

'Yes. I have,' a young scholar volunteered. 'There's a ghost story set in a place called the Castle of Shadows. I remember the author's note in the front said the castle was based on a real castle. I think it's in northern Orupee.'

'Could you check for me?' Kira asked. 'It's very important.'

'Of course. I'll do it at once.'

Northern Orupee! thought Kira. That's not far. If he's right, we could reach the next orb within two or three days. Kira reached out with her mind. *'Fang? Can you hear me?'* she called, concentrating all her will on reaching out through the bond. Nothing. Not a whisper. She felt no sense of his presence at all. *'Fang? Have you seen any sign of night dragons?'* Still nothing. He was out of range of her thoughts. He and Firestorm had been gone a long

189

time. Were they still bathing in the sea? Kira's instincts began to twitch again. Something was wrong.

Chapter Sixteen
A Fistful of Spears

As Aurora descended in a gentle arc to land in the meadow near the campsite the riders had used before, Elian's mind was elsewhere. He was trying to picture the Castle of Shadows. It would take about two days to fly there, but once they reached it – what then? They could not retrieve the orb without Kira, so was there any point in going there? If only they had not got separated, the penultimate step of the quest would be firmly in sight . . . if only.

Aurora refused to talk about the castle. If dragons deliberately avoided it, then it was obviously not a place to wait around in. There had been a distinct sense of dread through the bond when she told him of its reputation.

Pell had suggested returning to their old campsite for some breakfast and Elian was happy to oblige, though he was not sure if he should be eating breakfast or supper.

They had left through the dawn gateway from Isaa into France. Despite the journey taking an instant, they had arrived in the other world just before dusk. He had then been awake all night, as his body still felt it was daytime. At dawn in France, just as he was ready to rest, they had opened another gateway. This time they arrived before dawn in the mountains of Orupee. His eyes felt tired, as if it were late evening, but the day was just beginning. It was weird and disorienting.

As they landed behind Shadow and Pell, a movement between the trees caught Elian's eye. It took a moment for his mind to process what he was seeing and another for him to react.

'LOOK OUT!' he yelled at the top of his voice. 'THE TREES!'

Both dragons and Pell turned as one. It was too late to avoid the volley of weapons totally, but Elian's warning saved the dragons from certain death. Aurora could not dodge the first spear, but instead of it striking the middle of her body, it hammered into the muscle high on her right foreleg. The piercing agony of it lanced through the bond. Elian clutched his right bicep, as the muscle burned with an empathic shock of pain.

For a few heartbeats the air was full of weapons. Aurora swept her tail around to protect her torso as three more spears thudded home into the dense muscle along its length, sending further shocks of pain down Elian's back. Aurora opened her great jaws and roared with anger and pain. It was a primeval bellow that would have sent any normal foe scrambling for safety, but the hunters did not retreat. Even as he clutched his right arm with his left, another spear brushed the tops of Elian's thighs, whistling past with deadly momentum, whilst a further weapon lodged at a shallow angle across the nape of Aurora's long neck.

Shadow had also taken several hits. Her heavy natural armour had deflected some of the weapons, but one was caught under the leading edge of her right wing where the main muscle joined the wing to the body. Two more had penetrated her tail, which she too had instinctively used to protect herself.

'*Shadow! No!*' Aurora's mental cry to her fellow dragon reverberated through the bond, sounding deafening inside Elian's head.

The night dragon was incensed. She opened her mouth and let out an ear-splitting scream of defiance. She was preparing to strike back.

'*It's a trap, Shadow. Don't do it,*' Aurora

continued. '*They want us to fight back. Come. Follow me. We need to get away now. Can you still fly?*'

Elian did not hear Shadow's reply, but her posture changed and he could tell that Aurora had got through to her. He was surprised to have heard Aurora's words spoken to Shadow. He normally only heard her voice when she was directing thoughts at him through the bond.

'*Good. Follow me. We need to get out of their reach.*'

It was strange to hear just one side of the conversation, but Elian felt more than able to fill in the blanks. Aurora broke into a launch run, her powerful back legs driving away from the danger at a formidable rate of acceleration. Elian felt spikes of pain as the spears bounced with every muscle movement. Her gait was awkward as she tried not to put too much weight on her right foreleg, but she got up to flying speed quickly and was soon powering up into the air.

Once airborne and climbing away with a steady rhythm, Elian looked back over his shoulder to make sure Pell and Shadow were following. They were, but Shadow was struggling to fly with the spear stuck in her right wing. It was obvious they would not be able to go far. Further back, Elian could see the hunters bringing horses out

194

from between the trees. It seemed the men on the ground would not give up now they had drawn blood.

'How bad are your wounds, Ra?' he asked, leaning over to look at the spear sticking from her right foreleg.

'Bad enough, but they will not cause lasting trouble if we can draw the weapons soon,' she replied.

Elian's arm, neck and lower back throbbed with sympathetic pain. He did not know how she could make her mental voice sound so casual given that she had a fistful of spears lodged in various parts of her body.

'I don't understand, Ra,' Elian admitted. 'If those are the same men who attacked us before, why are they so set on hunting us? I thought they'd give up after seeing Shadow eat their leader, Kasau.'

'I am not sure I understand, either,' Aurora replied. 'Most dragonhunters do it for the money. There are those who will pay vast amounts for dragonbone, but this feels different. I don't think their new leader is entirely human.'

'Not entirely human? What do you mean?'

'There is something strange about his mind,' she said, choosing her words carefully. 'Kasau, their old leader, felt the same way. I have entertained a suspicion ever since our first encounter, but have been reluctant to mention it until now. If I were to make a guess, I would say their leader is a joining.'

'A joining? What's a joining?'

Aurora thought for a moment before answering. 'Explaining a joining is not easy,' she admitted. 'Humans name them differently around the world. The man looks normal on the outside, but there is a race of unseen creatures, bodiless and often malevolent, that can only express themselves by invading and using the minds and bodies of others. I think one of these creatures has joined with the leader of these hunters.'

'Demons!' Elian breathed. 'You're talking about demons,' he added with more volume. 'Are you saying he's possessed?'

'I've heard humans use this expression when talking about joinings,' she admitted. 'It is not an entirely accurate description, as the person who has been invaded still has limited control over his mind and body. The "demon", for want of a better name, will normally encourage behaviour in the host body that furthers its own agenda. A joining enjoys abilities beyond those of normal humans, but the relationship between host and hosted is not symbiotic. The spirit creature is very much a parasite. Any benefits the host body gains are granted only to further the aims of its invader and are often self-destructive.'

'If Kasau was possessed, did the demon die when Shadow ate him?' Elian asked.

'No, the spirit creature part of a joining cannot be harmed in that way,' she said. 'It will have transferred itself to another host body in the instant of Kasau's death. I expect it pre-selected him as the best available host. Demons have ever harboured a deep hatred for dragonkind. This one must have begun trailing us from the moment we first met. When Kasau led the dragonhunters into attacking our campsite that night at the meadow, he was expecting two dragons. The presence of Firestorm and Shadow took him by surprise.'

The thought of being selected as a host for a demon sent a shudder down Elian's spine. He was still coming to terms with the sensation of his bond with Aurora, but the idea of something invading him and taking over his mind was repulsive.

'Do not worry, Elian. Your mind is safe whilst I live,' Aurora assured him. 'One of the reasons these creatures are hostile towards dragons is that they cannot invade our minds. Once the bond is in place with a rider, you become immune to their abilities. If I am killed, you will become vulnerable, but I am not in a hurry to die just yet.'

'I'm glad to hear that.' Elian's stomach churned as

he considered what might have happened if he had not spotted the first hunter making his throw. He looked back to see where the others were. 'How is Shadow doing?' he asked. 'That spear in her wing doesn't look good.'

'She is struggling,' Aurora admitted. 'I have felt better, too. We cannot go far. Shadow needs to land and have the spears removed soon, but we also need to get as far from those hunters as we can. The joining will push his men relentlessly. No doubt they are being fed dreams of wealth. Little short of death will deter them now. However, most dragons do not kill except as a last resort.'

'What about Shadow eating Kasau?' asked Elian. 'The hunters were running away when she did that. That was hardly a last resort.'

'True,' she said. 'But Shadow is not like most dragons.'

'You. Here. Now!'

Husam barked out the order like a military drill instructor. His accusing finger singled out the man he was addressing. The hunter looked over both shoulders, half hoping the hunt leader was pointing at someone behind him.

'Yes, you!' Husam snapped, his strangely mismatched eyes narrowing with anger and his finger now pointing at the spot on the ground he wished the man to occupy.

Tembo watched in silence as the man Husam had singled out stepped forwards. The unfortunate hunter's eyes were wary and his face was draining of colour. Husam waited, motionless until the man was standing right in front of him. The rest of the hunters shuffled about uneasily. Those who had known Kasau remembered how intolerant he had been of error. Husam now had the same strange discolouration in one of his eyes. Would he demonstrate the same brutal code as the silent hunter had before him?

'You did not wait for my command. You threw early and drew their attention,' Husam accused, his body stiff with anger.

'Did I? I thought—'

'No, you did not think!' Husam interrupted. 'If a whisper of thought had entered your mind, you would have known to hold your position until I gave the word. If you had not been so impatient those dragons would be dead or at the very least, mortally wounded. Thanks to you, we're now faced with a long chase. Give me one good reason why I shouldn't kill you where you stand.'

The man did not answer. His face was white and his hands were trembling. Tembo eased forwards slowly, searching Husam's face for signs of his old friend. He was not the man who had set out with him from Racafi. This Husam was different. Something had changed him. Somehow he had inherited Kasau's cold aura. Husam had always been focused, but never with the burning intensity that he was displaying now. The change had come immediately after Kasau's death. What had happened that night?

'No answer?' Husam prompted. A blade suddenly appeared in his hand so fast that Tembo did not even see him draw it. The point was underneath the man's chin and pressing against the soft flesh there in the blink of an eye. Tembo was taken aback. For a moment he thought Husam was going to slit the man's throat. Taking another step forwards, Tembo clamped one of his huge hands over Husam's wrist.

'Enough, old friend,' he said. 'He made a mistake. If you want to punish him, expel him from the group. There's no need for this.'

'You're right, Tembo,' the slim hunter replied. 'He's not worth staining my blade on.' He lowered his knife and sheathed it again. His eyes stared into those of the other hunter with unblinking intensity. Sweat was pouring down the man's forehead. 'This is your first and final warning. Disobey me again and I will not hesitate. The same goes for the rest of you,' he added, projecting his voice with more power.

The men understood perfectly. It was the sort of language they expected from a strong leader. They were not shaken. Rather they looked galvanised into a stronger team. Tembo noted the reaction and was forced to question his own response. Was he imagining things? Was Husam playing a role to impress the men? His head told him it was possible, but his heart spoke differently.

'Bring the horses into the open and let's get going,' Husam ordered. 'They won't have gone far. If we're quick we can still end this today.'

'How do we know where to look?' one of the hunters asked, braving Husam's attention as he grabbed the reins of his animal.

'Finding them will be no problem,' Husam replied, his voice strange and resonating. 'I know exactly where they're going.'

Chapter Seventeen
Followed

Kira prowled back and forth like a caged tiger as she waited for the young scholar to return. Her eyes glowered dark thoughts and her right hand continually strayed to the hilt of the hunting knife at her belt. Everyone else gave her plenty of space.

Time and again Kira's eyes strayed back to Kalen's body and her lips tightened into a thin line of controlled anger. Should they mount a hunt for the killer? Should she and Nolita go looking for their dragons? Should they look for more answers here in the library? All appeared to offer danger of differing degree.

It was ironic that Nolita seemed more in control of her emotions than she was. The situation seemed dire. Kalen's murderer might still be loose in the library. The air was thick with tension. Night dragons might be nearby and somehow involved in Kalen's death, yet Nolita looked comparatively at ease.

'At last!' Kira muttered, as the young man returned clutching a tatty old book.

'Here it is,' he announced, waving the book in the air. '*The Castle of Shadows.*'

She intercepted him and pressed him to show her the map. Nolita and Conrad were not far behind.

'Here,' he said, opening the front cover and turning to the first page.

Sure enough, there it was, labelled clearly with a little image of a castle. It was on the northwestern coast of Orupee. Kira fixed the image in her mind and knew that she would be able to recall it at will.

'Conrad, why do you think Kalen considered this castle to be a place where shadows dwell?' she asked. 'Our quest leads us towards such a place, but we do not have time to go chasing fantasies. Why would he have been drawn to this book?'

'Perhaps it's due to the rhyme at the bottom of the map,' Conrad replied, pointing to four lines of writing at the bottom of the page. 'Look, it reads:

'*Come hither all darkness, come hither to death,*
Be still all ye living, if still ye want breath.

Here shadows await thee, fell creatures of Hell,
Come join us in shadow, for here shadows dwell.

'It's all nonsense, of course, written by the author to enhance the feeling of ancient evil and to set the mood for the book.'

'It sounds just like the Oracle's rhyming,' Nolita observed, a nervous note in her voice. 'I don't like the sound of it one bit. There is a resonance here that gives me the horrible feeling it might hold more truth than we would like.'

A chill had run down Kira's spine as Conrad read the verse. She agreed with Nolita. This sounded *exactly* like the Oracle's rhyming. Their path seemed clear. The Castle of Shadows beckoned, though the invitation to 'come join us in shadow' was not one she relished accepting.

'Thank you,' she said, her mind made up. She gave a slight bow to both Conrad and the young scholar. 'We must go. The killer has made his intent clear. He does not want us to get to this castle. I suspect I know who is behind the murder, though I do not wish to prejudice any investigation with my own suspicion. The race is on, Nolita. We had better get on our way as quickly as we can.'

'Wait!' Conrad ordered, his voice taking on the unmistakeable tone of authority. 'You are not clear of suspicion in this murder. I know I was with you at the time Kalen was discovered, but I judge he was stabbed some time before you joined me in the central area of the main library hall.'

'We ate lunch in the market street just to the west of the main courtyard outside,' Kira replied. 'No end of witnesses can testify to the time of our meal and our walk back. The scholars at the door spoke with us as we entered the library on our way to you. Given the interest people took in us, you will find us easy to dismiss as suspects. I'm afraid we can't wait around for the conclusion to any investigation. Our enemies are here. We must leave, or there will be more death.'

'Is that a threat?'

'No, Conrad. It's a fact,' Kira said firmly. 'Our enemies have shown that they will stop at nothing to prevent us completing our quest. We must go. I can't communicate with my dragon at the moment and I don't know why. I've got a terrible feeling that unless we get out of here now, all hell will break loose. Trust me, you wouldn't want that to happen.'

The old scholar looked her in the eyes. Kira met his gaze with unwavering calm. After a moment he looked away.

'Go,' he said. 'I see no evil in you. Go swiftly.

When the High Lord's enforcers get here and see Kalen's body, things will get very complicated. Ride well, and may justice ride with you.'

'Thank you,' Kira said, giving another bow. 'Come, Nolita. Let's go.'

Kira set off at such a pace that Nolita almost had to run to keep up. They threaded between the great labyrinth of bookcases, through the central study area and out the other side, following the meridian line overhead. For all her speed, Kira moved with no more noise than a breath of air. She was alert at all times, her head constantly on the move. When they reached the main doors she paused.

'Fang,' she called silently. 'Can you hear me?'

'Yes, Kira,' Fang answered. 'I'm here.' His voice sounded distant, as if he were right on the edge of communication range. It also echoed, as it had the night Fang had got them into the night dragon enclave. He was shielding his voice against being heard by other dragons, she realised.

'We need to get out of here. There's been a murder in the library. I've got a feeling that Segun is closing in on us. We need to get away quickly.'

'You're right about Segun,' Fang confirmed. 'Firestorm and I left in a hurry when we sensed Widewing and other night dragons coming. There are three of them in Harkesis. They are at the High Lord's palace.'

206

'Why didn't you warn us?'

'We tried,' Fang said, sounding guilty about his failure. 'I shielded Firestorm and we slipped away, but we were never close enough to be able to speak to you. We could not risk coming back to the Grand Library. They would have sensed us for sure. I imagine Segun is expecting us to come back and get you. Let's not make life easy for him. Meet me down at the beach. And try to make sure you're not followed. We don't want night dragons on our tail from the moment we get airborne.'

'Very well. We'll see you there.'

Leading Nolita down the great steps, Kira set off across the courtyard in the opposite direction from the beach. She moved at speed, projecting an air of purpose, as if she knew exactly where she was going. Anyone trying to follow would have to move swiftly, too. Kira did not look back. She needed to get out into the streets to start laying traps for anyone who sought to track her.

'Where are we going?' Nolita asked in a low voice as they reached the cover of the colonnade.

'I'll tell you in a bit,' Kira replied, her voice even softer than Nolita's. 'First, we need to see if we are being followed. Don't look back!' she added quickly, as she sensed Nolita's head beginning to turn. 'A good tracker will take precautions to prevent us seeing him.'

Kira indicated an upcoming exit and Nolita led the way through the archway and out into the street beyond. They emerged into the market street not far from where they had eaten lunch. Kira took the lead again, guiding Nolita to the right and along the length of the line of stalls. She moved effortlessly through the milling people like a fish brushing through fronds of weed on a riverbed, sometimes touching them, but not slowed by their presence. Nolita was not so slick. She bumped into one person after another, apologising for her clumsiness time and again, before they finally reached the last stalls and the clearer street beyond.

They continued along this street a short way then turned left into a narrow alleyway that led downhill towards the centre of the city. Nolita eyed the dim alley with suspicion. Even in broad daylight it was easy to imagine murderers or thieves lurking in such a place. With a gentle guiding push, Kira steered her in. Rats skittered along the edges of walls and darted into dark corners.

Kira glanced back along the alleyway as they emerged from it, but nothing was moving. The street contoured around the side of the hill, in both directions. Kira took them right and then turned quickly left down a short side street before turning left again. Ten minutes later she had led them in a convoluted loop, back to the market street outside the Grand Library.

As they rejoined the crowd, Kira took Nolita gently by the arm and led her across to a stall that was selling cheap jewellery.

'I don't think anyone is following us,' she said softly. 'But I want to make absolutely sure. As a hunter, I don't appreciate being stalked by someone.'

'I don't understand,' Nolita admitted. 'Why would anyone follow us?'

'Segun's here,' Kira said, picking up a wooden necklace and making a show of looking at it. 'And I'm sure he knows exactly where we are. We've not made a secret of our visit.'

'But how did he follow us here?' Nolita asked, instinctively looking for signs of the night dragons in the sky. 'Fire didn't sense them behind us. Did Fang?'

'No,' Kira said, shaking her head and putting the necklace back on the table. She leaned close to Nolita and continued in a low voice. 'How he did it is a mystery, but he's here and we need a way out. He's unlikely to move openly against us, as the High Lord of the city would be obliged to get involved if he did. Fang explained that the rulers of big cities hold dragonriders in high regard, equal to that of lords and ladies. But whilst we're here in the city, we're subject to city laws like everyone else.'

'So who do you think is following us?' Nolita asked. 'Not Segun, surely!'

'No. More likely one of his lieutenants – or he may have paid one of the locals to keep an eye on us. If it's a local, we're less likely to lose him, but it'll take him time to report back to Segun. If it's a rider, he'll have instant communication through his dragon, which will make things more difficult. Fang is waiting for us at the beach. We need to get down there and away from Harkesis before Segun has a chance to react.'

'How far is it to the beach?'

'About half a league, I think.' Kira pursed her lips. 'Far enough to be a problem – look! Try not to stare, but do you recognise that man over by the pig roast? He looks different without his flying gear on, but I'm sure that's one of Segun's riders.'

Kira continued to make a show of looking at the jewellery while Nolita turned to look up and down the market stalls. She did not let her eyes linger on the man, but her expression changed subtly as soon as she saw him. All remaining doubts in Kira's mind fled. He was a night dragonrider.

Kira and Nolita exchanged looks. They both understood the situation instantly. Kira thanked the stallholder for letting her look at his wares and the two girls walked calmly along the street away from Segun's man.

'What do we do now?' Nolita muttered.

'Well, as our jaunt through the side streets didn't lose him, I don't think we're likely to shake him off by trying to be clever,' Kira replied thoughtfully. 'He probably suspects we're onto him now, so I think the best thing we can do is . . . run!'

Chapter Eighteen
A Tricky Landing

Elian flinched at Shadow's hiss of pain. His dragonbone sword was clumsy and oversized for the
delicate task of removing the spears, but he had
no choice. Metal knives struggled to cut through
dragon flesh. At least the sword did so cleanly.

'Keep going,' Pell told him. 'You're nearly there.
Shadow knows you're not deliberately causing
more pain.'

It was a messy job, and it would get worse.
This was the first spear and his hands were slick
with Shadow's blood. They did not have long.
The hunters were already in sight, but Elian felt
relatively safe for the moment. They had landed
high up on a ridge and it would take the hunters
some time to reach them.

The spear came loose with the same horrible wet

sucking sound he remembered from the time he had drawn the spear from Fang's thigh. His stomach turned. He had nothing with which to stem the flow of blood flooding from the hole in Shadow's side. All he could do was to hope that none of the spears had hit major blood vessels, or the bleeding would not stop. He could not even cauterise the wound.

'Thank you, Elian!' Pell said, his voice thick with relief. 'I couldn't have done that.'

'Have you got any spare cloth, Pell?' Elian asked, deliberately changing the subject. He had never seen Pell show this sort of emotion and he found it embarrassing.

Pell thought for a moment. 'I've got some spare clothes in my pack.'

'Grab whatever you're happy to live without, fold it into a pad and press it over the open wound. You'll have to wait for the worst of the blood flow to stop. I don't have any medicinal herbs to help form a clot, so it might take a while.'

Elian ducked under Shadow's extended wing and walked back along her body, leaving Pell to scrabble through his pack for something suitable with which to plug the wound. Continuing around her tail, Elian reached the first of the two spears lodged there.

'*Shadow either got lucky, or she has tougher scales*

than you, Ra,' he observed. *'Your wounds look a lot deeper than this.'*

The first weapon had not penetrated far through the surface, but it was wedged tight. He moved along to the second. Again the wound looked superficial. The spear he had taken from the underside of Shadow's wing was by far the worst. Her armoured scales must be weaker there.

'Shadow's injuries will give her more trouble than mine,' Aurora said.

'Why? Have you got healing abilities that I don't know about.'

'Of a sort. Not in the same way that Firestorm heals, but enough that once the spears are out, I will regain my strength quite quickly.'

'That's a relief,' Elian admitted. *'I was worried about how much blood you might lose from five deep wounds. I've got no way of sealing them. How much time do I have to work on Shadow? The spears look as if they're going to be tricky to remove.'*

For the slightest moment, Elian felt as if his mind were soaring out from his body and flying down into the valley below. The sensation stopped abruptly, and he staggered as mind and body reconnected like stretched elastic snapping back to its resting state. He was about to ask Aurora what had happened, but realised he did not need to. The

214

bond between their minds had grown so strong that he often found his thoughts mixing with those of his dragon. Their minds were becoming ever more intertwined. She had mentally reached out to try to find the dragonhunters and had inadvertently taken his mind along for the ride. The sensation had been alien and he had instinctively retreated from it. What if he had relaxed and gone with her? What would that feel like?

'*You have about a quarter of an hour before we'll need to move again,*' Aurora said, interrupting his train of thought and bringing him back to the real world. '*We'll just have to keep hopping ahead of them until we can fly more freely. Let's hope the wound under Shadow's wing doesn't restrict her too much, or we may have to start looking for ways to slow the hunters down.*'

'Quarter of an hour!' Elian muttered aloud through gritted teeth. 'They aren't giving us much breathing space, are they?'

Aurora did not answer. Elian knew from her silence that he should focus and get on with what needed to be done. Pell was on the other side of Shadow, so he tilted his head back and called over to him.

'Tell Shadow to brace herself. I'm going to start on the second spear.'

'Go ahead. She's ready.' Pell's voice sounded

strained. Elian understood perfectly what he was feeling.

Elian decided to take out the spear embedded in the thicker part of Shadow's tail first. Gripping the shaft close to the wound, he tested the weapon's resistance with a steady pull. He hoped he might be able to just pull it straight out, but after a small initial movement the spear held fast.

There must be a barb under the scale, he realised. The only way to get it out would be to cut a path for it through the hard surface. The problem was identifying where to cut. The barb could be on any side of the spear – or there might be more than one. The spear tips Elian had found after the previous attacks had all been subtly different. He was kicking himself now for not having taken them away from the meadow and disposed of them. By leaving them where they had fallen, he and his companions had effectively rearmed the hunting party with their original weapons and given them a second chance.

Elian probed each side of the entry wound with the tip of his sword in an effort to identify the barb. Shadow flinched a couple of times and Elian did not want to imagine what his efforts must feel like. Having explored the wound as best he could, he decided where he needed to cut and sliced through the scale with the tip of the sword. Even though the blade was made of pure dragonbone, the scale resisted his efforts. He was sweating profusely when he finally managed to ease the spear free.

Moving swiftly to the spear further down Shadow's tail, he repeated the process. Although trying to be gentle, Elian was aware of the time it was taking. Aurora did not say anything. He could almost feel the hunters getting closer.

The last spear came loose with unexpected suddenness, taking Elian by surprise. He fell backwards onto the ground, crying out as he fell.

'Are you all right?' Pell called.

Elian brushed himself down. He was more shocked than hurt.

'I'm fine,' he called back. 'Shadow's all done.' He picked up the two spears and ran around Shadow's tail and under her wing to where Pell was still pressing a large blood-soaked wad of material against her wound. 'That'll do, Pell. We need to get out of here. The hunters will be on top of us any minute. Is she able to fly again?'

'She says she can, but I don't think she'll be able to fly far,' he replied.

'Good enough,' Elian said. 'Let's get away. Her other two wounds aren't serious. They'll hurt, I'm sure, but they're not bleeding badly. Come

217

on! Mount up. I don't want to have to cut more of these out of her hide,' he added, brandishing the two wicked-looking weapons.

With a final wave of the spears, Elian broke into a run to cross the short distance to Aurora. But there was one last thing he had to do before they left. Throwing the weapons down on the grass, he sliced through each of the long wooden shafts just above the dragonbone tips with his sword. The shafts he left where they lay. The tips, he collected. Sheathing his sword, he slipped his arms through the straps that held the scabbard across his back. A few more long bounding steps and he was scrambling up Aurora's uninjured foreleg and into his saddle. He tucked the spear tips into his saddlebag and buckled down the cover, barely finishing before Aurora leaped forwards and hurled herself into the sky.

They set off not a moment too soon. Even as they took to the air, the hunters crested the ridge and launched a volley of weapons. Elian held his breath as they hurled their spears. His heart was thumping, but none came close.

The hunters shrank to tiny figures in the distance almost before Aurora had settled into a steady flying rhythm. Aurora's present speed was about three times that of a galloping horse. In theory they should outrun the swiftest of hunters with ease, but in their present state the dragons could only fly for a matter of minutes before they needed to rest. Also, each launch sapped the dragons' strength more than all the time they spent flying. The acceleration and strength required to get off the ground was tremendous and the strain would be particularly telling on Shadow, whose injury would be tested with every launch.

Elian looked for her. Force of habit made him look above and to either side, but he eventually spotted Shadow quite a long way below and behind. She was struggling to maintain height and was barely level with the top of the ridge from where they had launched. His stomach tightened. Her wingbeats looked awkward and off balance.

'Can Shadow keep going, Ra?' he asked, sending his feelings of concern through the bond.

'Not for long,' she answered. 'The pain in her right wing is making it impossible for her to fly properly. It's a miracle she's airborne at all.'

'What about you? I'm sorry I didn't have time to care for you straight away, Ra. You know I wanted to.'

'I know you did, Elian,' she responded, her voice warm and reassuring. 'You did the right thing. The wound under Shadow's wing was the priority. Mine can wait a little longer.'

'But I can feel your pain,' he said, speaking his thoughts aloud. 'I know how much it hurts.'

'*You can also feel that the pain is bearable,*' she pointed out. '*I am strong, Elian. Normally I would say that Shadow is the stronger dragon, but as you can see, it is she who is struggling. We must stay focused on getting away from the hunters. If we can reach the Castle of Shadows that's where they will lose heart.*'

'Why there?' Elian asked.

There was something Ra was not telling him and he did not like the idea of secrets between them – especially when it came to their quest. He tried to look into her mind to see what she was holding back, but he could sense nothing other than a deep unease.

'*The Castle of Shadows is not its only name,*' Aurora said, her voice uncharacteristically bleak. '*Some call it the Castle of the Dead, others the Dark Keep. But most know it as the Castle of Despair. I would say this final name suits it best. If the hunters follow us in, there is no telling how the castle will treat them. One thing I will guarantee, though – joining or human, they will not enjoy the experience.*'

A cold clamp of dread tightened inside Elian's stomach. The Castle of Despair – just the name caused a blanket of depression to settle over him. His heart became leaden in his chest and for a moment it felt as if someone had attached weights to his limbs. His entire body was suddenly heavy with weariness.

A rising pocket of air caught under Aurora's wings. The sudden bump caused Elian's stomach to lurch and his hands to clutch the pommel handle with a white-knuckled grip. The jolt startled him and his mood lifted. It was with a certain amount of amazement that he realised how familiar the air rush and the rhythmic motion of riding on Aurora's back had become in the space of a few short weeks.

He looked down at the countryside sliding by below him with fresh eyes, and the wonder of it filled him afresh. It was hard to imagine ever being totally at ease when flying in turbulent air, but he had already become so comfortable in smooth conditions that he no longer even thought about how high he was above the ground. How long would it take before turbulence would also become second nature?

They flew on for about ten more minutes, keeping to the valleys and holding their height. The mountains to either side were lower than those around the area of the Oracle's cave, but they were still too high to consider climbing over with the dragons in their present state. When Aurora spoke again, she did so with deep concern in her voice.

'We're going to have to land,' she told him. 'Shadow can't go any further. She's going to try to land on the top of that ridge ahead.'

Elian could see instantly where Aurora meant. There was a spur jutting out from the side of one of the mountains. Towards the top there was an area of dense woodland, but the majority of the spur seemed to be grass-covered, with just a few occasional boulders jutting up like broken teeth.

He looked back at Shadow and then forwards again at the ridge. The night dragon would have to climb at least a hundred spans to land on the top. Would she make it?

Aurora was flying level with the top of the ridge as she approached. She stopped beating her wings and used her momentum to glide the final few dragonlengths. Elian had learned to trust her judgement and the final tilt of her wings combined with two powerful strokes brought them to a light touchdown.

No sooner had Aurora landed, than she turned to watch and encourage Shadow. Elian could feel his dragon urging Shadow on, but she was never going to make it to the top of the ridge. Despite her awkward-looking wingbeats, she had gained some of the height she needed. She was flying approximately fifty spans below the top of the ridge, but she seemed intent on landing.

It was only in the final moments of her approach that Elian realised what Shadow was attempting to do. Aurora broke into a run back across the grassy ridge to keep Shadow in sight as she began to disappear out of view under the nearby horizon. Elian hung on tight, trying to cope with the unusual motion. Normally when Aurora ran with him on her back, she had her wings extended. With her wings folded back her running motion was totally different. It felt unnatural, but he was as anxious as his dragon to watch Shadow touch down.

The night dragon was trying to land on the steep upslope, a short walk from the ridge top. To land there would be difficult for any dragon, but to try it with a wing injury seemed foolishness of the highest order. For a brief moment Elian thought the huge black dragon had executed the impossible to perfection, but as Shadow swooped upwards to parallel the slope her right wing collapsed with the strain of the manoeuvre. She rolled, crashing into the slope and ploughing to an abrupt stop on her side with her wing folded back awkwardly.

Pell was thrown clear on impact. He flew, tumbling head over heels through the air and landed on his back, disappearing into the dense heather.

To Elian it was as if the landing had happened in slow motion.

'Pell!' he called out, driving out the breath he had been instinctively holding. 'Pell? Are you all right?'

There was a pause and then Pell's head eased up over the tops of the heather.

'I've felt better,' he called back. 'But I'll live.'

Chapter Nineteen
On the Run

Kira raced through the market at speed. She was pleased that Nolita was quick to follow her lead. The day dragon rider was fast and fit.

Running through the streets of Harkesis was not like running through the deep grass of the savannah. In some ways it was easier, for she did not have to pick her feet up high to avoid getting tangled in the long grass. When hunting in Racafi, the sprint for the kill was almost a cross between skipping and bounding along. Here in the streets it was easy to accelerate, weaving through the thinning crowds, and then speed up into a flat-out sprint as they reached the open streets.

A glance over her shoulder revealed that the man they had seen in the market had abandoned stealth and was in open pursuit. They must have caught him by surprise with their sudden acceleration, as he was a long way behind them. Kira had no intention of letting him catch up.

'We need to get . . . to the other side . . . of the Grand Library,' she told Nolita, speaking in bursts that matched her breathing pattern. 'Fang is waiting . . . at the beach.'

'All right,' Nolita replied.

Nolita was regulating her breathing well. Kira had not seen the Cemarian girl run before, but if anything, Nolita was running more easily than she was.

'You run well,' Kira said.

'Thanks,' Nolita replied. 'I've always liked running.'

For several minutes they ran at high speed, turning along streets that would take them to the left and around to the far side of the huge library building. By the time they had circled the hilltop to the western side, their skin was glistening with a sweaty sheen. The man was still behind them, but he had not managed to close the gap.

Kira was not sure what it was that made her look up. It might have been a whisper in the air. It might have been a movement in the corner of her eye. Whatever it was, the sight of the night dragon approaching from the north set her pulse racing even faster.

'Quick!' she gasped. 'It looks like . . . our friend back there . . . has called for help.'

She pointed and Nolita's eyes widened as she followed the line of Kira's finger and saw the approaching dragon. Her face paled with fear and her stride lengthened still further as the sight spurred her on to even greater speed. Kira found that she had to accelerate to keep up as Nolita's burst of fear-driven energy drove them forwards.

The city was spread out below them like a leprous white scab on the countryside. Beyond the edge of the city the sea sparkled with an intense blue that seemed almost unreal. Kira looked down to where the strand of dazzling white sand awaited. The line where the white buildings stopped and the blue water began seemed little more than a stone's throw away, yet Kira knew that appearances could be deceptive.

Leading Nolita around the corner to the right, Kira began to descend the hillside towards the sea. Allowing their downhill momentum to carry them forwards at speed, the girls found that running became both easier and more difficult. Easier because running fast required less effort, but more difficult because keeping the speed under control became a balancing act. Lean forwards too far and the body threatened to overtake the legs. Lean back too far and the momentum was lost, or their feet slipped out from under them.

The dragon powered closer, racing across the city like a gigantic black angel of death.

'This way!' Kira gasped, pulling Nolita to the left and into an alleyway. The dragon swept overhead with great whooshing wingbeats, its talons trailing so low that they were almost dragging across the rooftops. No sooner had it passed than it entered a gentle turn to the right that carried it westwards, soaring out over the lower terraces of the city.

The girls reached the end of the alley and turned right, as if to head down the hill again, but no sooner had they turned than Kira grabbed Nolita's arm and skidded to a stop. She held a finger to Nolita's lips, working hard to control her own breathing and keep it as silent as possible.

The man was approaching fast. They could hear his footsteps coming closer and closer. Kira timed her strike perfectly. Just as he reached the end of the alley she stepped out, bending her right leg and pivoting on her left so that she drove the point of her right knee directly into the stomach of their pursuer. He folded over as if made of paper, all wind driven from his lungs. Before he had a chance to fall, Kira clenched her right fist above her right shoulder and drove her elbow up into the man's face in a rising strike that caught him right between the eyes.

Nolita's eyes were wide with shock, her fear of the dragon momentarily forgotten as Kira attacked. The elbow strike was most effective. The rider collapsed to the floor and remained there, unmoving.

'Where did you learn that?' Nolita asked. 'Is it a hunting trick?'

'Not exactly,' Kira said, grabbing her companion by the hand and starting off down the hill again. The pace this time was slower: more of a jog than a run. 'It was frowned upon by my tribe . . . if a woman got into a fight. One of my fellow hunters . . . did teach me . . . a few basics, though. Get in close. Use the hard points of the body: knees, elbows and heels. We girls might not have the power . . . or muscle bulk of the men . . . but we can still be . . . effective fighters.'

The night dragon had not yet completed its lazy turn, but it suddenly let out a deafening screech that sent people all over the city running for cover. The anger in the dragon's cry was unmistakable.

'Uh oh!' Kira muttered, dragging Nolita into another side alley and into the shadows. 'I think perhaps I . . . might have been a bit rash. Hurt the rider – anger the dragon.'

They stood still. Waiting. Kira grabbed both of Nolita's arms and looked her in the eyes. The night dragon's cry had filled the girl with paralysing fear. Kira could feel her shaking. Damn it, she thought. I'm doing this all wrong.

'Don't be frightened,' she panted, giving Nolita an encouraging smile. 'We'll get out of this. Trust me . . . Fang is waiting. It's not far now . . . We'll be out of here in no time. Come on . . . Keep the night dragon out of sight . . . If we can't see it – it can't see us.'

It was not quite true, of course, but Kira did not want to complicate her statement with exceptions. The dragon swept overhead again and the two girls pressed themselves flat against the wall of the alley. The light dimmed momentarily as the shadow of its great wings passed over them. Then it was gone. The dragon cried out again, but this time its voice appeared to be keening. There was a note of anxiety in its cry that under different circumstances might have pulled at Kira's heartstrings.

'Go! Go!' she urged, pushing Nolita along the alley. 'We need to use every moment of cover we can.'

A second dragon's voice cried out. The tone of this one was totally different from that of the first. Kira sprinted past Nolita and into a shadowy doorway, waving Nolita in to join her. Another night dragon! The net was closing in fast. If any more night dragons took to the sky, the girls would not be able to wiggle a little finger without one of the dragons seeing it.

'Fang?' she called silently. 'It's getting difficult to move up here. Is there any chance you can divert the attention of the night dragons?'

'I can get their attention easily enough, Kira,' he replied. 'But once I have it, I'm unlikely to be able to help you again for a while. The light is too bright for my camouflage to fool them once I'm on the move. If they give chase it's likely to take me some time to lose them. There is no cloud and nowhere to hide.'

'All right, that's not a good idea,' Kira said. 'Any suggestions?'

'Confusion is your best weapon,' Fang replied. 'Night dragons have amazing perception at night, but during the day it is possible to fool them.'

'How?'

'Use your hunter's instinct, Kira. You're used to being in their position. Apply what you know in reverse.'

Although it was nice to feel Fang's confidence in her abilities, Kira would have preferred a direct suggestion. Confusion? How could she confuse them? Her thoughts flashed back to past hunting trips. What had she found most confusing? As she had become more experienced at stalking it had become rare for her to lose track of her prey, but in the early days there had been many times when a hunt had taken turns she did not expect. The second dragon passed overhead, wheeling out over the lower tiers of the city.

'Come on, Nolita,' she said, an idea forming. 'We need to keep moving. Follow me.'

For the next ten minutes they ran, twisting and turning through side streets and alleyways. Kira doubled back on herself frequently, but always looked aimed to progress downhill towards the coast. She stuck to narrow streets and alleys to limit the dragons' ability to see them, and also to prevent them from trying to sweep down and snatch them into the air.

'We're nearly at the coast, Kira,' Nolita panted. 'And we haven't lost them. Widewing's up there as well. They'll be guiding the riders to us.'

'Not far now,' Kira said. 'Don't lose heart, Nolita. I know what I'm doing.' Silently she added: *I hope.* Nolita was terrified as it was. There was no point making it worse for her.

They reached the end of the narrow street. A strong odour of fish filled the air. Ahead was an open square. On three sides of the square were houses, but the fourth was open, bordered only by the street that ran along the shoreline at the top of the beach. Around the square was an open-air fish market.

Table after table was piled high with every sea fish imaginable, shaded from the sun by bright striped canopies mounted on poles. Lots of people were wandering along the lines of stalls. Merchants with their rich clothes and feathered caps mingled with the poor. Fishermen, brown-skinned from long exposure to the elements walked alongside scribes and would-be scholars. Sellers in their wide-brimmed straw hats and blood-spattered aprons touted their wares with loud voices. The smell of the fish was intense, but almost pleasant in comparison to the foul stench of the rest of the city. Kira stopped, catching Nolita and pulling her into a doorway before she ran out into the open.

'Listen!' she said urgently. 'This is what we're going to do . . .'

Picking her moment, Nolita sprinted across the short distance to the nearest stall, slowing to a normal walk as she joined the streams of people who were mingling around the open market. Kira waited a few moments and then walked slowly out from the narrow street and into the open, scanning the sky above for the dragons. They had climbed. Two were circling directly above, whilst the third was still circling some distance away near to where she had tackled the rider who had followed them.

She moved past the line of stalls and into the centre of the square. At least one of the dragons was watching her. She could feel its gaze. As she moved out further into the open, so the other dragons turned their focus on her as well. Kira did not flinch. She continued to walk calmly into the open until she was standing in the middle of the square, clear of all the main activity of the market. There were a few people criss-crossing the centre of the square, but most were around the long lines of tables at the edges.

One dragon turned and descended westwards out over the sea in a wide looping turn. Kira tracked it with her eyes, taking an occasional glance back up at the dragon still circling directly overhead. They were clever. The one above was watching to see she did not make a run for it while the second positioned to come in and grab her.

In her mind, Kira kept repeating the same words over and over. She knew dragons could pick up surface thoughts, so she fed them what they wanted to hear. *'I'm done with running. I'm done with running. I'm done . . .'*

Turning to face the approaching dragon, she watched as it dropped lower and lower over the water until it was racing in off the sea towards her. The people around her seemed oblivious to it. She imagined that the dragons had attracted attention when they first appeared in the sky over the city, but now people had become comfortable with their presence. The approaching dragon loomed large as it swept in across the beach. Its talons were extended forwards, ready to pluck her from the square.

For a moment, Kira thought she would have to scream, but just as she opened her mouth, sporadic yells and screams from around the square triggered the wave of panic she had anticipated.

'DRAGON ATTACK!'

Sudden realisation dawned. People all across the square scattered, fleeing for cover. Kira joined them, delaying her run until the last possible instant in order to draw the dragon in as close to the market as she dared. She darted left initially, racing under a green-and-white striped canopy and emerging on the far side wearing one of the wide-brimmed stallholder hats. Nolita had jammed it onto her head as she passed, joining her as they both zipped up one of the nearby streets, carried along by the wave of people.

The dragon let out a roar of frustration as it pumped its wings to climb away from the square.

The roar added another level to the panic and the wind generated by its great wingbeats blew several of the canopies over, taking the tables with them and scattering fish over the ground.

Even as they ran, Kira spotted another night dragon rider in the crowd ahead. He was trying to move against the flow, his anger etched in deep lines on his face. Kira tugged Nolita's sleeve to catch her attention and the two of them swept by him with their heads down, faces shielded by the broad brims on their hats.

During the next few minutes, Kira and Nolita swapped hats several times with passers-by to further confuse the searching dragons and their riders. There were a few startled protests as the swaps were made, but no one reacted fast enough to stop them. Kira also acquired a cloak that had been dropped by its owner. By the time they had circled around to the beach, Kira was confident that the night dragons and their riders had lost track of them.

Through familiarity with her dragon and the pull of the bond, she could feel where Fang was waiting. Although she could not see him, she knew he was close to the sea wall, no more than a dozen paces from where they were hiding at the end of a narrow alley. The final run would be a gamble. If they were seen, all their efforts would have been in vain.

'Here we go, Nolita,' she whispered. 'On three: one, two, three . . .'

Hearts thumping the two girls raced the final few paces and vaulted over the wall, dropping two spans to the sand below. They landed with a simultaneous thump into the soft sand and rolled to a stop, breathing hard. Kira looked up and saw two of the night dragons still circling. For a moment she thought they were exposed and would surely be seen, but then the air above her shimmered. Fang had covered them with his wing. She relaxed. As far as the city was concerned, they had just vanished.

'Kalen? Murdered? In the Grand Library?' Lord Tarpone sat down with a thump as he stared at the messenger. 'But who would do such a thing? He's an academic. He wouldn't hurt anyone.'

Segun watched as the messenger bowed and departed and he allowed himself an inward smile. This was working out better than he had planned.

'It is as I said, my Lord,' he said smoothly, his deep voice full of regret. 'The renegade riders are a danger to your people. They may look like innocent young girls, but their appearance only serves to make them all the more dangerous. I've just had word from my dragon that my men are currently pursuing them through the streets towards the western quarter of the city. Do not fear, my Lord. I will see them brought to justice for this crime.'

'Are you sure it was these girl riders who killed Kalen?' Lord Tarpone asked, sounding surprised. 'What makes you so certain?'

'It matches their previous behaviour pattern, my Lord,' Segun replied. 'The fact that they're running from the scene strengthens the likelihood of their guilt. When was the last time anyone was murdered in the Grand Library? I find it highly unlikely that it could be anyone else. They are ruthless. Especially the darker of the two.'

'But what possible motive could they have?'

'Motive? My Lord, these girls don't need a motive. As I told you, my men and I have been pursuing them for some days now. Be assured, we will catch them. And when we do, justice will be swift. It is the dragonrider way.'

Chapter Twenty
Making a Stand

Shadow did not look well. She was holding her right wing awkwardly against her side. Once she was sure Pell was uninjured from his fall, she climbed the final few dragonlengths to the top of the spur and lay down to rest.

'Is Shadow going to be all right?' Elian asked Pell as he began the gruesome task of removing the spears still sticking from Aurora's body.

'She will be if she's given time to recover,' Pell answered. 'But we both know that's unlikely. What are we going to do, Elian? She can't fly in this state.'

'She might have to unless we can dissuade the hunters from following us,' Elian said, easing the tip of his sword into the first wound and using it to feel around the head of the spear for barbs.

'Dissuade them?' Pell asked, incredulous at the

idea. 'How can we dissuade them? They don't want to talk. All they want is to kill our dragons so they can cut them up and sell them. They're barbaric!'

'Who said anything about talking?' Elian said, pausing to give Pell a wicked grin. 'Aurora thinks one of them is possessed. She calls him a "joining". If she's right, they are unlikely to give up even if we could talk sense to them.'

'A joining!' Pell breathed, his eyes widening. 'There are stories of joinings told in Isaa, but I thought they were the stuff of nursery tales designed to keep young children in line. You know: "Don't be naughty, or one of the devil's children might think you're ripe to become a joining".'

'Well, it seems they are something more than that,' Elian said, twitching with pain.

It was weird trying to tease the spear from his dragon's foreleg, whilst feeling empathetic pain in his own arm. He tried to twist the spear free, but the spike of pain that shot through his arm stopped him.

'*Sorry, Ra!*'

'*Don't worry, Elian. I can stand the pain, if you can. You need to get the spears out quickly. The hunters will be pushing hard to catch up with us. I'd like to be ready for them. I see in your mind what you're going to propose to Pell and I agree. It is the only way.*'

240

'Thanks, Ra,' he said gratefully. '*I'll do my best to get it over with quickly.*'

By probing with his sword, he knew there were no barbs on this spear. It was just the depth of the wound and the spontaneous contraction of the muscle around it that was holding it fast.

'What are you planning, Elian?' Pell asked. 'There are only two of us, and I saw at least ten of them.'

'There are four of us,' Elian corrected. 'And we are holding the high ground. I think we should try to make a stand here, even if it is only a brief one. We need them to see that we're not going to let them kill our dragons without a fight.'

'All right, you'll get no arguments from me on that count,' Pell said. 'But what can we do against so many?'

'Help me get these spears out and I'll show you,' Elian promised. 'Grab the shaft here and pull when I say. It will probably help if we twist it to the right at the same time. I may not be able to pull with my full weight because of the pain through the bond, but don't stop. It should come out cleanly if we pull it hard enough. Ready? Pull!'

The lancing spike of pain that tore through his arm caused him to cry out and tears filled his eyes. His right hand lost grip on the shaft, but he gritted his teeth, twisted and braced his back against Aurora's leg so that he could continue to help Pell by gripping the shaft from below and pushing the spear outwards with his left hand. The spear tore free suddenly and Pell staggered backwards. No sooner was it clear of the wound than Aurora's scales around the area of the wound began to glow from within.

A flood of blood from the open wound spilled over Elian's shoulder, but the flow was short-lived. A curious burning sensation began in Elian's arm where the sharply defined pain had been just a few seconds before. It spread, heating his entire upper arm with a sensation that was not quite pleasure and not quite pain. Unable to resist, he rubbed at the arm to try to disperse the intensity of the experience, but it made no difference. The fire continued to rage until he felt sure his flesh must be melting.

As suddenly as it started, the burning dissipated to a gentle tingling throb.

'*That's better,*' Aurora announced, her head arching around on her long neck and her tongue darting across the site of the wound. '*Thank you. Do you think you could draw the others now?*'

The spears in Aurora's tail came out without too much difficulty, but the one in her neck proved more awkward. Although lodged at a shallow angle, it was hard to get at the wound. The solution was to have Aurora lie on her side so Elian could stand on her neck and pull the spear free. It had particularly nasty barbs, which made the process very messy.

Each time he and Pell took out one of the weapons, Aurora's scales around the wound lit up and Elian felt the sympathetic burning sensation as she healed the flesh under the surface. The wounds stopped bleeding straight away and the residual pain was much reduced, which helped Elian to stop worrying about her.

'Look!' Pell said suddenly, drawing Elian's attention from his dragon. He was pointing back along the valley. 'The hunters again! I can see them in the distance.'

'Already? Damn!' Elian cursed. 'I would've liked more time, but we'll just have to make do.' He turned back to Aurora. *'Do you think you can manage a bit of lifting and dragging?'*

'Yes, Elian,' she replied. *'I'll manage. How many do you think we'll need?'*

'I don't know, but we should try to set as many as we can,' he said. *'We don't have long. Do what you can. I'll get Pell to help me find some smaller stuff.'*

Aurora rolled up onto her feet and stretched out her neck. She turned her head and looked along the valley to where the hunters were just visible in the distance, and she snorted. With that she moved off over the ridge until she was out of sight of the hunters and turned right towards the woods.

Elian grabbed Pell by the arm. 'Come on,' he urged. 'There's no point in staring at them. Help me get ready. We need to collect rocks – hand-sized – the more, the better. There's plenty of loose stuff over here.'

'What are we going to do? Throw stones at them?' Pell scoffed, standing his ground. 'You think that's going to make them go away? They're not children, Elian.'

Elian paused a moment and glared at Pell. 'Have you ever been hit by a stone that's the size of a man's fist, Pell?' Elian picked up a comfortably-sized piece of stone and walked to the top of the slope. 'Watch,' he said. With that he hurled the stone off the edge of the ridge, sending it upwards at an angle of about thirty degrees and watching as the stone arched through the air to strike the slope a long way down. 'From up here, not only is our range huge but with the momentum the stones gain in the long drop, they will fall like deadly hail. The hunters aren't wearing armour and they'll be inside our range long before we're in theirs. The stones will give them pause for thought. Ra has gone to get us some larger, more lethal weapons.'

Pell looked unconvinced, but he followed Elian to an area of rocky ground, where there was some loose material for them to scavenge. Before long they had a small pile of suitable ammunition – enough for about a minute of rapid throwing.

When Pell saw what Aurora was doing, his eyes widened and his body language suddenly became a lot more positive. By the time the hunters reached the bottom of the ridge about a half hour later, the two boys were sweating profusely, but there was fire in their eyes. They watched the hunters dismount, leaving one man to look after the horses. Spreading out in a line, they began their long climb up the slope towards the waiting boys.

Shadow had not moved in all the time they had been working. Her injured wing twitched from time to time and Pell cast frequent worried glances at her.

'Will she be able to fly again today?' Elian asked. 'We'll not hold them off indefinitely, you know.'

'I know,' the older boy sighed. 'She tells me she feels able to fly, but we won't really know for sure until she tries. I feel her pain. I'm not sure she's being honest with herself. That landing earlier hurt more than she's willing to admit.'

'What do you think, Ra?' Elian asked silently. 'Will Shadow be able to fly today?'

'She will have to, Elian,' his dragon replied. 'Shadow knows this. For all that she's in a lot of pain, she has deeper reserves of strength and endurance than most.'

Elian looked across at the enormous black dragon and he hoped with all his heart that Aurora was right. Pell could be a pain at times, but Elian had no desire to see him or his dragon fall prey to the hunters. He drew a deep breath and held it for a moment in an effort to calm his nerves. Fourteen men were climbing the slope, with a fifteenth visible down in the valley. This last one was leading the horses around the end of the spur in anticipation of a further journey. He would be out of sight soon, but it would not do to discount him completely.

'Right, Pell, you take the men to the right and I'll aim for the ones to the left,' Elian said decisively. 'Remember, we need to get them to bunch together so Ra has a more compact target. She will help us as they get closer.'

'I'll do my best,' Pell replied. 'Good luck.'

The two boys picked up a stone in each hand and waited. They had tried throwing a handful of rocks at different angles to get a feel for their range, so the moment the hunters came close enough they let fly with their first stones. Once they had started, they did not stop. They stooped again and again to pick up further ammunition, launching a continuous barrage at either end of the line.

Most of the stones missed their marks, but Pell got lucky with one, a flattish rock that spun, twisting through the air in a curve that the unfortunate hunter did not predict. It caught him on the shoulder, smashing down with such force that it snapped his collarbone like a twig. He fell, yelling and clutching at his shoulder. As Elian had hoped, the line began to contract, the men instinctively closing together as the rain of stones dropped like bombs from the sky.

Aurora timed her first strike beautifully. Almost at the instant Pell's rock struck down the man at the far right, she appeared at the crest of the ridge. Heaving the heavy load between her jaws, she whipped it out and over the edge, using every last scrap of power and leverage her long neck offered.

Distracted by their colleague's cry, the men did not see the enormous tree trunk coming until its first ominous wooden thud reverberated through the ground under their feet. To begin with, the tree did not so much roll down the hill as gambol, making it doubly difficult to evade. Two men were hit full on and another was struck a glancing blow as he attempted to dive over the top of it. Elian had used the dragonbone sword like an axe to remove the branches. The blade had passed through the thick branches like a knife slicing soft cheese. Once the trunk was in motion, it bounded down the slope, accelerating at a frightening rate.

A few seconds later, Aurora hoisted another tree trunk into the air. The last remnants of the hunters' line disintegrated as the second enormous projectile hurtled down the slopes. Chaos reigned. Some of the men began to retreat. Others accelerated, trying to press home their attack. The remainder dithered, or were injured.

The hunters' confusion was a thing of beauty. Elian picked up more stones to rain down upon them, sending rock after rock in a steady stream, but he was running out fast. Pell's pile was almost gone too. Aurora swung her third and final tree trunk, aiming it at the men still moving forwards.

'Time to go!' Elian called across to Pell.

The two boys raced to their dragons and leapt up into their saddles with practised ease. Aurora waited for Shadow to lead. The great black dragon let out an ear-splitting shriek of defiance at the hunters before racing across the spur and hurling herself off the far edge. Her wings spread to catch the air beneath their vast span and she sailed from the ridge into the sky. Elian held his breath. For one horrible second it looked as though Shadow's injured right wing would fold under the strain. She wobbled dangerously, but quickly steadied herself and gently began to beat her wings with a reassuring rhythm.

'Ready, Ra?' he asked. He felt her eagerness through the bond. *'Let's go.'*

Following Shadow off the ridge, they launched into the sky. To Elian's surprise, however, Aurora did not follow the black dragon for more than a few wingbeats. Instead she dipped her left wing and began to descend in a fast gliding arc down into the valley below.

'What are you doing, Ra?' Elian called aloud. The pain of her wounds was all but gone as far as he could tell through the bond. There was no reason he could think of for her to be descending.

'I'm going to make it more difficult for the hunters to follow us this time,' she replied.

The wind tugged at Elian's hair as they continued to accelerate in the long curving turn. Suddenly Elian saw her target – the horses. Of course! he thought. It's the perfect opportunity.

He squinted his eyes and leaned low to Aurora's back as they dived faster and faster. The horses were quick to spot the approaching dragon. The solitary man leading them fought to keep control as they bucked and reared with fear. He was thrown to the ground as the horses pulled in every direction, each trying desperately to get free from the chain.

Aurora lifted her talons into their strike position and grabbed at the lead horse, lifting it into the air with a lurch and tossing it into the rest of the line. Many of the horses were bowled over. Elian felt sorry for them as he and Aurora soared upwards in a steep climb into the sky. The poor animals were simply in the wrong place at the wrong time. But this was no time to get sentimental. Shadow was unlikely to be able to fly far. Aurora turned on a wingtip, reversing direction and diving back in for another pass.

The man in charge of the horses saw what was happening and decided enough was enough. Live horses were more useful than dead ones. With a flash of steel he drew his sword and slashed at the rope that held the horses together, running through an iron hoop on each set of reins. Those horses that were still on their feet suddenly found they were free. In a matter of seconds they scattered like chaff, galloping away at a speed born out of panic.

Aurora passed over, driving the horses away. She circled, spooking the horses still further and forcing them to run fast and far. Shadow was little more than a speck in the distance when Aurora began the long chase to catch her up.

'That should do it,' she told Elian, sounding pleased. 'The hunters will eventually round most of them up, but the horses will be tired and fretful for some time. If Shadow can fly even a modest distance, the hunters won't catch up with us again today.'

Chapter Twenty-one
The Castle of Despair

This place felt a world away from the white city of Harkesis, yet only three days had passed since they had eluded the searchers and slipped past Segun and his men. The forbidding grey stone of the sea fortress and its imposing skyline gave notice to those who approached from land or sea: expect no welcome here. Even from the air the gigantic structure looked grim, cold and empty. The enormous gates on the landward side of the castle stood open, but there were no flags flying from the solid square towers. No people walked on the thick, crenellated walls. As Kira and Fang flew over the great structure, she saw the inner courtyards were bare of any signs of life. Where were the people who built these monstrous defences, and who were they so afraid of that they should expend such resources on a castle of this size? A prickle ran up her spine and the skin on her arms rose in a rash of goosebumps.

The wind was blowing hard from the southwest, whipping the sea into a frothing frenzy of foam-tipped waves. Great streaks of white ran across the grey water in long streamers. Sea birds whirled and dived above the cliffs, their mournful cries rising and falling in tones that ached with loss. Thick cloud scudded overhead, an endless racing ceiling of grey driven across the sky by the blustery wind. Spits and spots of moisture carried on the gusts, but the clouds seemed in too much of a hurry to drop any organised rain. The dim light made the air feel thick with the onset of night, yet it was barely past midday.

Across the wide estuary to the north, Kira could just make out the shadowy outline of a second large sea fortress.

'Are you sure this is the place, Fang?' she asked. 'There's another castle on the other side of the water.'

She knew the answer to the question before Fang replied, but she clutched at the grain of hope that she might be wrong. The Castle of Despair, he had named it. She was already beginning to see why.

'This is the castle we seek,' Fang confirmed, his voice sounding as bleak as the gulls'. 'We need to *land in front of the gates. To try and land within the walls in this wind would prove treacherous.'*

The seaward side of the castle was flush to the sheer cliff, which dropped a hundred spans straight to the rocky beach below. On the landward side, there was a broad area of open land all the way around the castle – a killing ground, stripped of cover and designed to leave any enemy brave enough, or mad enough, to assault the fortress vulnerable to the weapons of those within. A road from the castle gates ran due east across open land and disappeared under the trees of the nearby dense forest. Aside from this large area of open ground, the countryside for miles around was tree-covered, with only the occasional hill crowns emerging like isolated islands in a dark green sea.

They descended in a skidding arc, the wind carrying them sideways and then slowing their forward speed over the ground as they continued turning until they faced head on into the wind. When they touched down they were barely moving forwards at all and they came to a stop in a few skipping steps. Kira dismounted, leaning into the gusts as she walked the short distance to meet Nolita. Her companion's blonde hair was streaming across her face.

'It's a bit wild, isn't it?' Kira commented, shaking her head to allow her own hair to catch the wind.

'The wind, or the castle?' Nolita answered, squinting up at the great grey walls with narrowed eyes.

'Both. What do you think? Should we go in?'

'I'd feel happier if the boys were here,' the blonde girl admitted. 'No disrespect for your skills, Kira, but I felt safer when we were travelling as a group of four.'

'You can tell Nolita her wish is granted,' Fang said suddenly. *'The others are coming. Look south.'*

Kira looked. Sure enough, two dragons were approaching. They were flying low across the tree-tops. One was clearly the orange-gold colour of a dawn dragon. The other was larger and black, but was flying awkwardly. If it was Shadow, then something was wrong with her. Kira grabbed Nolita's arm and pointed.

'W . . . What?' Nolita spluttered. 'How?'

'I don't know,' Kira said, watching Aurora and Shadow turn to make their landing. 'But I'm glad to see them. If Segun shows up now, we'll have a fighting chance of standing up to him.'

The two dragons swept around in a tight turn and landed nearby. For once, the fear that Nolita normally displayed in the presence of dragons was replaced by a look of relief and genuine delight. Kira was not sure whether to be pleased by Nolita's lack of apparent fear, or hurt that her companion did not find her company sufficient.

The boys slid to the ground next to their dragons and the girls ran to meet them.

'How did you . . .' Kira and Elian began simultaneously.

Kira, Elian and Nolita laughed. Pell's face remained serious. Elian ignored him.

'Ladies first,' he said, giving a little bow. He then gave each of the girls a brief hug. 'It's good to see you – Kira . . . Nolita. Come over here. Let's use Ra as a shield from the wind. I don't want to have to shout.'

Pell came with them as they moved behind Aurora, but he stood to one side, his face expressionless.

'Well, after you abandoned us to Segun and his men . . .' Kira started. Elian raised his hand and opened his mouth to protest, but her quick wink made him realise she was teasing. 'It took us a while to throw him off our tracks. Fang suggested we might find the answer to the riddle in the Grand Library of Harkesis, but apparently Segun came to the same conclusion. I'm not sure who reached Harkesis first, but that doesn't really matter now. A scholar called Kalen was helping us with our search. We think Segun had him murdered. Once we realised the night dragons were in the city, we ran for it. Kalen told us about the castle with his dying breath. I'm surprised we haven't seen Segun yet. He could turn up at any moment.'

'He's already here,' Pell said, his voice flat. 'He's hiding in the trees over there with Widewing.'

'What!' Kira exclaimed, looking to where Pell was pointing. 'Fang? Is he right? Is Widewing in the trees?'

There was a pause and she could feel her dragon reaching out with his mind.

'*Ah! Yes, she is there with Segun,*' he replied, sounding apologetic. '*She is keeping well hidden. I don't sense any others with her, though.*'

'It must be a trap!' Kira said aloud, her body tense and her mind racing through options. 'How many men has he got with him? We should get out of here! Now!'

'Don't panic, Kira,' Elian said calmly. 'I don't think he'll bother us at the moment. We're four. He's alone – for the moment at least. He sent his men into the castle a couple of hours ago and we've seen nothing of them since. Ra can't sense them any more. She says they won't return. In fact she's been saying a lot of gloomy things like that ever since she realised we were coming here. She seems genuinely scared of this place.'

'Yes, Fang and Firestorm are the same,' Kira said. 'The castle doesn't have a good reputation amongst the dragons. But how did you get here? How did you solve the riddle?'

'We didn't,' Elian said, giving her a broad grin and pointing over his shoulder with his thumb towards Pell. 'Pell forced the Oracle to tell us where to come.'

'He did!' Kira was amazed. 'How?'

'He threatened to smash the second orb if the Oracle didn't tell us.'

Nolita gasped. 'But you wouldn't have done it, would you?' she asked quickly.

'Yes. Actually, I would,' Pell replied, still without emotion. 'And I nearly did. I'm beginning to wonder if the Oracle is the force for good everyone says it is. Think about it. These orbs it needs – one sucked blood from Nolita, the second was formed from a dragon's heart. The first drew predators with its aura and the next killed indiscriminately every time night fell. They're hardly wholesome attributes. Why does the Oracle need these things? To regenerate, it says. To regenerate into what? Will it be the same creature when this regeneration is complete? Something about this quest feels wrong to me. What gives the Oracle the right to demand these sacrifices?'

'The second orb killed?' Nolita said, her face paling. 'Who did it kill?'

Pell did not answer. His eyes challenged the girls to answer his question first.

Elian broke the awkward silence.

'Look,' he said. 'We're here to get the dusk orb, and we should do it now. Segun isn't our only worry. We've spent the last four days fighting a running battle against dragonhunters.'

'More hunters!' Kira exclaimed.

'We think they're the same crowd as before.' Elian scowled as memories crowded his mind. 'Ra and Shadow have both taken injuries, but Shadow's are the most limiting. Her wing is badly hurt. They'll be close again by now. According to Ra, their leader is possessed.'

'Possessed? How?'

'An evil spirit creature has taken control of his body. She calls him a "joining". It seems joinings have a particular hatred of dragonkind, so they're not going to give up the chase. We're here. We came for the orb. Let's go get it, or do you want to abandon the quest after what Pell has said?'

Nolita looked unhappy and unsure. Kira was more decisive.

'No,' she said. 'Let's get on with it. We've come this far. Let's get the orb ... unless Aurora needs healing?' She glanced at Nolita for confirmation and then guiltily at Pell. It seemed unfair that Fire could heal all but his night dragon, but she could not change the facts. Nolita nodded agreement.

'Thanks, but Ra is fine,' Elian said gratefully. 'Her wounds are not troubling her at the moment.'

'In that case we should get the orb now before Segun gets reinforcements. I've got some questions that I'd like to ask both Pell and the Oracle, but they can wait. How many night dragons entered the castle?'

'Two,' Elian answered.

'We outnumber them. Good. I guess Fang and I should lead, as it's the dusk orb we're after this time.'

She looked across at Pell, expecting a challenge. His expression did not change and he said nothing. Kira did not quite know what to make of his silence, but it was Elian who spoke again.

'Why not have Fang and Firestorm lead the way?' he suggested. 'If we follow them on foot, Shadow and Aurora can bring up the rear. I'd feel a lot safer if I had friendly dragons all around me. Although the gates are big enough for us to ride our dragons inside, there's no telling where the orb is. If there's danger, the dragons will be able to move far more freely if they don't have us on their backs.'

Kira nodded and the dragons agreed.

It was further than it looked to the great grey gates of the Castle of Shadows. The wind whipped around them, howling over the battlements and moaning through the thin archers' windows with a keening so powerful that the riders could feel it in their chests. Kira stuck her fingers in her ears in an effort to block out the sound, but nothing seemed to dull its bite.

As they got closer, so the walls towered higher. The structure was truly gargantuan, its sheer scale making even the dragons seem small and insignificant. They reached the enormous arched gateway. Kira looked up and around. When she had been at the Grand Library in Harkesis it had been hard to imagine a doorway bigger than the main entrance there. That seemed laughable in the face of this gateway. This was a gateway for giants.

'Or worse,' Fang added.

'Worse?' she asked. 'What do you mean?'

'There is something here, Kira,' Fang said slowly. 'The castle may look deserted, but do not be fooled. We are not alone.'

'You're probably sensing the night dragons,' she suggested.

'No, it's definitely not the night dragons,' Fang replied. 'I have tried to sense ahead for them and I feel

261

nothing even remotely like the mental tones of a night dragon. What I feel is more transient. Something is leaking fleeting traces of thought – nothing identifiable, but there is a sense of watchfulness about the castle. Something is waiting.'

The wind strengthened as they walked through the great archway. It funnelled through the gap in the walls, as if trying to push them back. Kira's sharp eyes could just make out the lines of a huge portcullis hidden in a dark recess above them. She stepped more swiftly as they passed underneath it, her mind picturing it dropping with a great rumble. As they reached the inner end of the tunnel, the wind died away to little more than a swirling breeze. The noise of the wind in the battlements was still audible, but distant.

The inner keep stood squat and dense, dominating the central area of the castle. It had been built towards the southern side of centre, leaving a large open area at the northern end of the castle. Firestorm and Fang headed for the open area, keeping as much open space around them as possible. They were hunting for the orb, but Kira felt very much like prey here.

Several old trees, twisted, broken and long dead, stood within the walls. They seemed sad reminders of the life that had once lived within the castle. In their day, they must have been great pillars of colour and life, but their broken remains now only served to enhance the feeling of death and loss.

As they progressed across the open courtyard towards the seaward wall of the fortress, Kira began to sense the watchfulness that Fang had mentioned. Her hunter's sense was prickling. She could feel eyes following her. Her own eyes were constantly on the move, and her ears strained to hear even the slightest of sounds that might give a clue to where the watcher, or watchers were hiding. There was nothing. Only the noise of the wind and the gulls.

They rounded the corner of the inner keep and the two lead dragons stopped.

'What's wrong, Fang?' Kira asked immediately. 'Why have you stopped?'

'Don't move, Kira! Stand absolutely still. The other dragons are instructing their riders,' Fang said, his voice urgent. 'Whatever happens in the next few minutes, you must not move. If you do, you will die.'

Chapter Twenty-two
Demons and Traps

Kira froze, barely able to breathe. The sense of fear leaking through the bond shocked her. What had her dragon seen that could cause him such fear?

A movement caught the corner of her eye and she was tempted to ease her head around to the right to see what was there.

'*Don't move!*' Fang ordered again, reading her intention. His fear for her was so strong this time that any thoughts of looking around were shredded. '*Not even slightly.*'

The movement in her peripheral vision teased, whatever was there was coming closer.

'*What is it?*' she asked. '*What's there?*'

'*They don't have a name,*' Fang said. '*"Shadow demons" is the closest I can come to describing them. I should have recognised them when we entered, but for* some reason they escaped my notice until I saw the remains of the two night dragons.'

'Remains?' Kira tried to swallow the lump that formed in her throat. Her mouth suddenly felt dry and swallowing was not easy. She was not upset to learn that the night dragons were dead, but night dragons were not easy prey. It had taken a lot of griffins to kill Knifetail and that struggle had been noisy. Whatever had killed these two dragons had done it silently and so fast that the dragons had not had a chance to warn their leader, who was hiding not far away.

An itch began to tickle at Kira's nose. The wind was blowing loose hair across her face. She clamped her teeth together and tried to ignore it.

Another movement. This time she could just make out a shape.

The trees! she thought. It's the trees!

'There are no trees here,' Fang told her. 'The things you took to be trees are deadly creatures from another world. I did not see them as trees, but as piles of old stone. They have an uncanny camouflage skill not dissimilar to my own. I doubt the night dragons even saw them coming. My eyes see more than most.'

'So how do we get past them?'

A warm wave of positive emotion flooded through the bond in response to her question.

'I'm glad you did not ask about retreating,' he said. 'The best thing we can do with these creatures is to stand our ground and let them get used to our scent. If we remain still until they have dismissed us as a threat, we should be able to move slowly forwards and into the keep. The doors are open.'

The nearest tree creature was coming closer. Kira noticed a slight haze surrounding it. The blurring was subtle, but now that she knew the shadow demon was not displaying its true form she began to see where its camouflage was distorting reality. What was it like underneath the disguise? No sooner had the question raised itself in her mind than she realised she did not want to know the answer. She had the horrible feeling that if she were to see the creature's true form it would haunt her sleep for the rest of her life.

Kira could feel the shadow demons all around them now, yet they made no noise. It was as if they were gliding on cushions of air. Although their movements were smooth and without menace, Kira felt this was yet another part of their deception. A slight whimper from Nolita proved her correct. In the blink of an eye the creatures closed in. Their speed was terrible. Kira had never seen anything move so fast, except perhaps the strange spitting weapons of the other world where Elian and Aurora had taken them.

The tensing of her muscles was instinctive. Kira could not help it. She felt Nolita tense up beside her as well. The creatures loomed over them, not touching, but uncomfortably close and circling round and around.

Don't try to run, Nolita, she prayed. Please don't move.

Despite the cool wind, she felt a trickle of sweat run down her temple. Another tracked down her back underneath her shirt. The air bristled with fear. The dragons were projecting it in sharp spikes that stabbed through the bonds and the riders were frozen, muscles locked rigid with breathless terror.

For what seemed like an eternity they stayed that way. Frozen. Suspended in a whirling dance of deadly peril. How long they had been standing when she first felt the shift, Kira could not tell. The withdrawal was so gradual that she was not sure it was really happening. The relief, when Fang confirmed it, was immense.

'*They are pulling back,*' he said. '*Remain still. We should be able to move again soon.*'

Time seemed to flow with the reluctance of chilled treacle. When Fang finally said they could move forwards again, Kira realised she had no idea if one minute or a dozen had passed since the shadow demons had begun to pull away.

'Let's take it one step at a time,' he said. 'Make no sudden movements. Keep everything slow. Once we've crossed the threshold we should be safe. The creatures do not like to be inside.'

'Safe from them,' Kira amended. 'But who knows what awaits us inside? My hunter's instinct is prickling. This place is full of danger.'

Fang did not respond, but she could feel through the bond that he shared her worries.

They moved forwards. Keeping her movements painfully slow, Kira raised her hand to comb the loose hairs from her face with her fingers. The relief she felt as she scratched her itching nose was heavenly.

Near the main doors into the keep, Kira spotted the remains of the night dragons. If Fang had not identified the bloody masses as draconic, Kira would have had difficulty in working out what she was looking at. There was very little left. Trails of dark blood streaked the stones where the carcasses had been dragged to their resting places under the sea-facing outer wall. Of the two riders, there was no sign. Kira did not want to think about what had happened to them, but she felt sure they were dead.

Step by step, the dragons and riders moved forwards towards the doors. Fang stopped everyone twice more before they reached the entrance, but each time Kira only counted a few heartbeats before they began moving again. The doors into the keep stood open. They were big enough for the dragons to pass inside in single file. Fang went first, followed closely by Firestorm. The riders went next, followed by Aurora, with Shadow bringing up the rear.

Once over the threshold, the dragons and their riders relaxed. The sense of relief was quickly replaced with one of amazement. The large entrance hall seemed far bigger than its true dimensions as the walls were all mirrored. Endless reflections ran outwards to infinity, making it seem as if an army of dragons was lined up ready for battle.

'Strange,' Kira commented. 'Why would anyone want to mirror all the walls?'

'I don't know,' Elian replied, his voice filled with wonder.

'It's a trap,' Pell said bluntly, his knife drawn and his head turning slowly from side to side. 'There's no other reason I can see for it. I've heard of such places before. Mirrors can be made so they reflect on one side, but are as transparent as normal glass from the other. I sense we are being watched.'

'*Is he right?*' Kira asked Fang.

'Maybe,' her dragon replied. '*I, too, feel we are being watched, but I cannot sense anyone hiding behind the glass.*'

'Well,' Kira announced in a loud voice. 'Watched, or not, we're going to press on. If the orb is here, I'm not leaving without it.'

'Aren't we the feisty one?' a voice boomed, echoing in the hallway.

As one, the riders and their dragons looked around, searching for the owner of the voice. There was no sign of him.

'Come then,' the voice continued. 'Come and claim your precious orb. You do so at your peril.'

'Who are you?' Pell called, his words sounding thin and powerless by comparison. 'Show yourself.'

The voice did not answer. Nothing moved. All was silent again.

'It seems you were right about our being watched,' Kira observed, glancing at Pell and raising one eyebrow as she scanned the myriad reflections for anything that might hint at the location of the hidden speaker. 'At least he's confirmed we're in the right place. Let's keep moving, but we'd better take it slowly and carefully.'

Fang and Firestorm moved forwards along the hallway towards the far end. Their reflections approached them from the opposite direction. At

270

first it seemed the hall was a dead end, but as they neared the far wall it became apparent that there was another mirrored hallway leading off to the right. Fang turned into the new passageway.

It was darker in the side hall and narrower. With the two dragons ahead of them the riders could not see to the far end. The reflections on the sidewalls no longer echoed true images of the group, but twisted and distorted them in bizarre ways.

As Pell entered there was a whispering *swish*, followed by a very loud *thunk*, and all light was abruptly shut off.

'What was that?' Kira asked, her heart fluttering as she felt Nolita grab her hand in the pitch blackness. She gave her companion's hand a comforting squeeze. 'What happened?'

'Ra says another mirror dropped from the roof and sealed the entrance,' Elian said, his voice remarkably calm. 'She and Shadow cannot follow us.'

'But it's only glass!' Kira said, exasperated. 'Let's all move forwards so she can break through.'

'That was my first thought as well, but apparently she can't. She says the mirror has been coated with dragonsbane. She can't even get close to it.'

'*Dragonsbane?*' she asked, addressing Fang through their bond. '*What's dragonsbane?*'

'It's a particularly nasty poison,' Fang replied, his voice strangely subdued. 'It is harmless to humans, but to dragons it represents a terrible danger. Shadow and Aurora must not get close to the mirror, or they risk a horrible death.'

'If this stuff is so deadly to dragons, why don't dragonhunters use it?' Kira asked. 'Surely dragon-hunting would become a whole lot safer for them if they did.'

'Dragonhunters know nothing of it,' Fang replied. 'Dragons have kept the secret of dragonsbane for millennia. And even if they did know, they would not use it.'

'Why not?'

'Because a dragon that is poisoned with dragonsbane does not just die, it dissolves,' Fang explained. 'The hunter would have nothing to show for his victory. Even the dragon's bones lose their integrity and become useless mush. Dragonhunters rarely hunt just to make a kill. Most hunt for the gold. There would be little profit in killing dragons by use of dragonsbane.'

'Well someone has learned the secret,' Kira observed. 'Why do I get the feeling that the owner of that voice is toying with us?' she added aloud.

Golden light suddenly filled the mirrored hall, causing their twisted reflections to leap into life. Firestorm was breathing out a gentle flame.

'If he is, then he'll regret it,' Pell said, his tone cold.

Firestorm kept the flame going for some time before he stopped to draw breath. The reflections leered and gawped at them from both sides with impossible faces.

'We'd better keep moving,' Elian said. 'Ra says that she and Shadow will wait for us in the main entrance hall, but she wants to be out of there before nightfall. The shadow demons are at their most dangerous in the dark.'

'Can you move forwards, Fang?' Kira asked, speaking aloud for the benefit of the other riders.

'Yes,' he replied. *'I think the hallway widens ahead. It might be better for Fire to lead, as he is the only one who can light the way.'*

The dragons moved forwards so Firestorm could squeeze past Fang and take the lead. Fang let the riders pass him as well to restore the protection of a dragon in the lead and at the rear. Firestorm moved with great care, keeping his flaming breath alight for as long as possible. Before taking each step, he made a close inspection of the ground, walls and ceiling, looking for further traps. It was slow going, but little by little they progressed, following the hallway around to the left and then to the right.

273

Pell began to get frustrated. If given a choice, Kira felt sure he would gladly run the gauntlet of the mirrored corridors, gambling on his speed and strength rather than using the wits of those around him. He was a person of action who could not stand delay. She noticed him first begin drumming his fingers on his thighs and then bunching the muscles at his jaw as he gritted his teeth behind taut lips. Next the grumbling began. At first his muttering and mumbling was unintelligible, but gradually Kira began to pick up on snippets. When they reached the junction she was not surprised to see his patience dissolve completely.

'It's a simple choice!' he snapped. 'Turn left. Turn right. It doesn't matter which. Just choose one and be done with it!'

The mirrored hall had met another at a T-shaped intersection. Fire stopped to allow the riders a view of the options before turning.

'Not so fast, Pell,' Elian said, his eyes narrowed with thought. 'We should set a marker here. This has all the makings of a maze. Let's not get lost before we begin. Have we got any way of marking our path?'

'Hunters in my tribe normally arrange sticks on the floor in patterns to leave a trail,' Kira said thoughtfully.

'Genius!' Pell scoffed. 'And this place is littered with them, of course.'

Kira ignored him. 'We could use the same patterns but by scratching the mirrors with a knife. Here let me try. Let's start by going left.'

She drew her knife and moved to the mirror facing them at the head of the T. The point of the blade made a horrible noise as she carved her symbol into the glass. It was a blend of grinding and screeching that set teeth on edge and shivers racing up and down spines.

'Nice!' Pell commented. No one responded to his provocative tone.

Once Kira was content with her marking, Firestorm took the left path and set off again. The going was slow. The passage twisted and turned, but soon they met another T junction. As they approached it, Kira heard Nolita gasp and the blonde girl's hand tightened around her own.

'Kira!' she said urgently. 'Fire wants you to move to the front. He says there's something you need to see.'

Kira was surprised. Why had Firestorm specifically asked for her? She gave Nolita's hand a squeeze and then made her way around the bulk of Firestorm to the front. It took a moment for her to notice what had stopped the dragon in its tracks.

When she saw it her jaw dropped and she looked around in amazement.

'But . . . but that's impossible!' she exclaimed.

Chapter Twenty-three
The Impossible Maze

'Elian, Pell, Nolita – come and look at this!' Kira called, her mind reeling.

Her three companions came running. Firestorm's fiery breath ran out just as they arrived. All plunged into darkness as he drew in another. His fresh exhalation lit the mirrored hall again. Kira pointed at the scratched symbol on the mirror.

'Look!'

'So you drew another symbol!' Pell said sarcastically. 'So what?'

'That's just it,' Kira said softly. 'I didn't draw another symbol. That's the one I did last time.'

'It can't be,' Elian replied, shaking his head. 'That means we just walked a loop, but the first time we approached a T-junction we came along a passage with no other turnings. At least, I didn't see

277

any. Firestorm was careful. He would have stopped us if there had been a junction.'

'I know it makes no sense,' Kira admitted. 'But somehow we've come in a circle.'

'Maybe someone else is in here,' Pell suggested. 'The owner of the voice, perhaps. Maybe he saw the symbol you drew and copied it deliberately to confuse us.'

'If he did, then he's got an uncanny eye for detail.' Kira pointed at a point on the symbol. 'See here. I slipped slightly with the knife tip as I drew this bit. It would take amazing control to replicate that.'

'Well, let's not get tied up in knots over it,' Pell said firmly. 'Assume for now that turning left does lead in a loop. That still leaves the passageway to the right.'

Kira nodded. She took out her knife and added a couple of extra scratches to her symbol on the mirror, annotating the second direction. The riders moved back behind Firestorm and once again let him lead them slowly forwards, this time taking the other passageway. Several minutes passed as they carefully followed this second mirrored corridor through a convoluted series of turns.

Again Firestorm stopped when they reached a T-junction.

'Fire says there's a symbol scratched on the mirror ahead,' Nolita said, her voice worried.

'Let me see,' Kira demanded, pushing her way around Firestorm until she could see the mirror at the head of the T. Her expression hardened as she reached it. 'Someone's playing games with us,' she said coldly. There's no way that both left and right passageways can loop back here without there being another junction. It's simply impossible. Is there room for the dragons to swap around? I'd like to try reversing our direction and seeing where that takes us.'

Firestorm moved into the passageway to the left, while Fang went into the passageway to the right. Fire then backed up and headed back the way they had just come. The riders followed, with Fang at the rear again. A couple of minutes later they reached the same T-junction with the scratched mirror directly ahead of them.

'Now that really is weird!' Elian said, his voice sounding hollow and worried.

Pell scowled and Kira could see that Nolita was shaking. Kira said nothing. She was desperately trying to think of an explanation, but the mirrored passageways defied logic. The entrance from the hall of mirrors had sealed behind them. It should now be a dead end, yet all routes in this series of mirrored hallways appeared to lead to the same junction, each bringing them back to the same scratched mirror from the same direction without even a hint of another junction in sight.

Reaching through the bond, Kira sensed the mirrored passageways had Fang equally vexed. It was the first time that she had felt confusion in her dragon's mind since she had met him, but to her surprise there were no parallel feelings of worry. The dusk dragon was more intrigued than concerned. He liked puzzles and she sensed he found this to be a particularly good one.

'What do you think, Fang?' she asked.

'I think whoever built this place was uncommonly clever,' Fang replied, dodging the real question. 'I have a couple of potential theories, but nothing I would like to wager on yet.'

'Do dragons wager?' she asked. 'I've never heard that before.'

'There is a lot you do not know about dragons, Kira,' he replied. 'But you are learning – slowly. I would like to test something. We have encountered nothing harmful in the hallways, so I feel this has been designed as a containment trap. Assuming this is true, I'd like to send half of the party in one direction, while the other half go a different way. I know one group will be without light, but I suspect this will not be for long.'

Kira did not like the idea of splitting up. They were already separated from Shadow and Aurora. The mirrors were hiding something sinister. She had the distinct feeling that they were not alone. Would they meet the owner of the voice if they did as Fang suggested? Although she felt uncomfortable with it, she knew they had to do something.

'Fang says we should split up and try both left and right at the same time,' she told the others.

'What good will that do?' asked Pell.

'It will show us where the two passageways meet,' Elian answered quickly. 'Of course one team will have to walk the passages in the dark.'

'Fang doesn't think anyone will be in the dark for long,' Kira said.

'And can you explain why he thinks this is the case?' Pell looked sceptical.

'He didn't tell me,' she answered. 'But he does have a theory about what's going on.'

'Is it magic?' asked Nolita, her voice shaking almost as much as her body. 'Has someone put a spell on this place?'

Kira relayed the question to Fang.

'There is no magic at work here,' he said confidently. 'Dragons are both sensitive to, and immune to the effects of, magic. No. There is a logical explanation to these looping passageways. I've asked Fire to take *the left passage. Please tell Nolita and Elian to go with him. We'll take the right passage with Pell. Tell the others to tread lightly and listen very carefully as they go.'*

Kira did as she was told. Nolita looked relieved and flashed Elian a grateful smile as he caught hold of her hand and led her after Firestorm, who was already beginning to move slowly along the left passageway. Pell's expression was unreadable as he waited with Kira for Fang to lead the way into the passageway to the right. Kira was glad when Fire's light faded behind them, as the darkness provided a retreat from Pell's intense stare.

Fang moved ahead of them remarkably quietly for a creature so large. His talons made barely any sound on the stone floors. Kira made a fascinating discovery in the dark. She found she had developed something of a sixth sense. If she concentrated hard, she could feel exactly where Fang was at all times. The occasional click of his talons on the stone helped, but there was more to it than hearing. It was almost like seeing him, but in her mind, rather than with her eyes. On several occasions she reached out and found the tip of his tail exactly where she expected it to be. It was very comforting.

Pell did not share the silent attributes of his

dragon, Shadow. He blundered along, his breathing loud and his footfalls easy to pick out. When Kira first heard the whispering noise she thought it must be some sort of echo. It was only after hearing it for the third or fourth time that she became certain that the noise was coming from ahead, rather than being reflected.

'What is that?' she asked Fang silently.

'It is the corridor ahead,' he answered cryptically.

'The corridor?'

'Yes. I'll explain when we meet up with the others.'

Soon a faint glow became visible ahead. It reflected along the corridor, the light bouncing from mirror to mirror. Fang increased his pace and caught up with Firestorm, Elian and Nolita as they reached the same T-junction again. There were no other junctions.

Despite their silent approach, Elian sensed them coming and turned.

'This is ridiculous!' he exclaimed in frustration, putting his hands on his hips and frowning. 'How can it be possible?'

'Fang says he can explain it,' Kira said. 'I'll relay what he says.'

'It is actually quite simple,' Fang began, 'though the mechanics behind it are likely to be complex. This trap works on sequenced pressure. As we move along a *passageway, our weight on the flagstones is translated through mechanical means into signals that are raising and lowering certain mirrored panels ahead of us. The direction we are travelling dictates the sequence and in turn shapes the passageway that we meet ahead of us. Not all the mirrors move. Most have solid walls behind them. The trick is to find which of the mirrors are mounted on a false wall, and which, if any, conceal the way to the dusk orb. We should look to the flagstones, too. I feel it likely that the key is under our feet.'*

No sooner had Kira finished repeating Fang's explanation to the others than the voice they had heard in the main entrance hall spoke again, its booming tones echoing around the corridors.

'Well done!' the voice said. 'Well done, indeed! I never thought to see someone solve the mystery of the mirrors so quickly. You have a keen eye for detail, dusk dragon. I shall save you the trouble of smashing up my maze. It is difficult to find craftsmen who can make suitable replacement mirrors these days. Take the passageway to the left again. You will find the exit quickly enough. Do not tarry. Delay and you will die.'

'Wait!' Pell called. 'Who are you?'

'Pell is wasting his breath,' Fang commented to Kira. *'His presence has gone. I think I'm beginning to understand more than just the nature of this castle.'*

'What do you mean?' Kira asked.

'I believe I've solved the riddle of the orb,' Fang replied. 'We shall see if I'm correct when we meet the owner of that voice.'

Kira did not want to wait for an answer, but she could tell from Fang's tone that he would tell her no more at the moment. His voice had a grim edge to it. Whatever he was thinking, she was certain it was not pleasant. The natures of the previous two orbs resurfaced in her mind's eye. One filled with blood, another formed from a dragon's heart – what would make up the core of this orb?

> Ever protected, the dusk orb lies
> Behind the cover, yet no disguise.
> Afterlife image, unreal yet real,
> Lives in the shadows, waits to reveal.

Was the voice waiting to reveal the orb? It appeared to live here in the Castle of Shadows. If it was really waiting to reveal the answer, why was it playing games and setting traps? The rhyme still made no sense.

The hairs on the back of Kira's neck began to prickle.

'The voice wasn't bluffing,' she hissed in an urgent whisper. 'We're not alone in here any more.

Move! Quickly! Something's coming – and it's not friendly.'

The feeling that danger was approaching was more than intuition. Years of hunting in the savannah of Racafi had tuned her senses and refined her instincts. She could not say how she knew, but she *knew* they needed to get out of the maze as fast as they could.

Fang led the way forwards. The riders followed, with Firestorm at the rear. They rounded the corner and, as promised, a short way down the mirrored corridor was a large hole in the floor. The stone flooring had slid aside to reveal a set of stairs that were designed for a dragon to descend. The steps were too deep for the riders to step down, but they dropped down from step to step, Firestorm providing light with his breath.

Firestorm began his descent. No sooner had he fully committed to the stairs than a whispering grate of stone on stone began above them. It concluded with a soft *thump*. The opening into the mirror maze had shut. A warm flush of relief ran through Kira's body and the sensation of imminent danger dimmed to a glimmer. The tension drained out of her shoulders. Whatever had entered the mirror maze was trapped. Despite the fact they were being herded forwards with no control over their path,

Kira felt sure that an encounter with whatever was now in the passageways above would not have been pleasant.

As they neared the bottom, Kira felt a flutter of excitement in her stomach. A pile of unlit torches lay on the ground next to the bottom step. Each rider grabbed a couple of torches from the stack. Firestorm lit one of Elian's and he lit one each for the others. Kira climbed Fang's side and the others passed her up the spares, which she inserted, handle first into her saddlebags. They stuck out of the top, but she wedged them in place so they would not fall out. Then she climbed down to join the others.

The torches gave off an unusual scent, much like the musk candles that merchants from the Far East traded on markets all across Areth. The odour was warm and sweet, instantly raising images in Kira's mind. Not memories, but hints of dreams and daydreams; strange lands, balmy nights, exotic trees and birds with feathers of many bright colours.

The riders took the lead this time, walking with Fang just behind them and Firestorm remaining as the rear guard. The tunnel was wide enough for the dragons, and appeared to have been carved through solid grey rock, the colour of the castle above. The walls were rough-hewn with odd alcoves and holes where darkness clung until direct light exposed their empty interior. The orange light of the flickering torches made shadows dance and flee with swift, darting movements. More than once, Kira could have sworn she saw movements that were not shadows, but she was quick to dismiss them as figments of her imagination. She felt no warning prickle of danger and was sure that if there were anything alive down here that could hurt them, she would sense it.

'What was that?' Nolita whispered, coming to an abrupt halt.

'What was what?' Kira asked, dropping her voice to match Nolita's hissing whisper and scanning the passageway ahead for any sign of movement. She held her torch high, but nothing was in sight. Nolita's face was pale as milk and she was shaking again.

'It . . . I could have sworn . . . there was a dragon's tail,' she stammered. 'A black dragon's tail. I saw it whip away around the corner ahead. I think Segun has managed to get ahead of us somehow.'

'Nonsense!' Pell said immediately, but Kira was surprised to hear a note of uncertainty in his tone. Had he seen something, too?

'*Did you see anything, Fang?*' she asked.

'No,' he replied calmly. '*I sense there is a presence ahead, but it is not close enough to see.*'

'Relax, Nolita,' Kira said, placing her hand on the girl's shoulder. 'After the shadow demons and the halls of mirrors it's not surprising that our imaginations are running a bit wild. Fang assures me there's nothing there.'

'But I saw . . .'

'I saw something, too,' Elian admitted softly. 'I couldn't say what it was, but something is ahead of us. I definitely saw movement.'

Nolita looked at Elian. Kira found it hard to tell if Nolita was grateful for his admission, or terrified by it.

Pell had gone uncharacteristically quiet. The heady fumes of the torches coiled around them as they paused, filling the air with their musky scent.

'Let's keep going,' Kira suggested. 'We'll stay on our guard and be ready to let Fang and Fire take the lead, if necessary. Come on. It can't be far now.'

She took Nolita's hand in hers and led her onwards along the passageway. They had hardly walked a dozen paces before a roar from behind brought the four riders to an abrupt halt. A bright flare lit the tunnel as Firestorm belched huge jets of fiery breath back along the way they had come.

'What's happening, Nolita?' Kira asked, unable to see around Fang well enough to tell what Firestorm was doing.

'Fire says we're being followed,' she replied. 'He says he wants to let whoever is behind us know that we're in no mood for games.'

'Did he see who it was?' asked Elian.

'No, but he says he's been aware of them almost from the moment we descended the steps.'

'Shadows in front, shadows behind – the castle is doing its best to spook us,' Kira said, trying to sound brave, but no longer sure that she felt it. 'Well I'm not going to let figments stand in my way. We came for the orb. Are we still going in the right direction, Fang?'

'*As far as I can tell*,' he answered. '*I can't be sure, but my heart tells me we are getting closer.*'

'That's good enough for me. Let's get this over with.'

Chapter Twenty-four
Power that Binds

Kira led the way forwards, striding ahead at a bold tempo. She still held Nolita's hand and was all but dragging her companion along behind her. The boys followed, a couple of paces back. Elian looked uncomfortable, while Pell tried and failed to appear unconcerned.

The underground passageway continued in a gentle curving descent to the right. Shadows continued to dance and leap ahead of them, but Kira ignored them. Her head was aching and her eyes felt sore. The orb was close. She was sure of it. All she wanted to do was face whatever challenge awaited and get it over with. The rhyme did not hint at what sort of challenge it might be. Nolita's had been a test of bravery. Pell's had been a test of courage, skill and endurance. What challenge awaited her?

The slope grew steeper and the steady *plink, plink, plink* of water dripping into a pool seemed to echo unnaturally loud in her ears. Was that mist ahead? Underground mist? She had never heard of such a phenomenon. The wispy tendrils thickened until the entire passageway was filled with an unnaturally thick fog that reduced visibility to no more than a few paces. Barely slowing at all, Kira forged onwards into the murk and was gently swallowed up.

The slope flattened suddenly. Kira stumbled as her legs adjusted to the change. The passage straightened. A glance back over her shoulder and she could see Fang's great eyes reflecting the torchlight above the heads of her companions. She touched him through the bond and was reassured by his calm.

The torches began adding to the murky atmosphere, giving off grey smoke into the moist air. They guttered and spluttered, but continued to burn on stubbornly in spite of the damp. Where just minutes before, the sound of dripping water had rung around them like a bell, now all sound fell dead, muffled by the mist. The temperature tumbled. To the riders it seemed as if they had crossed another threshold into a different world – a dead world where nothing grew and the dark had strength to smother light. The shell of light around them shrank to little more than a fragile cocoon as they stumbled forwards, engulfed in stone and strangling fog. The four young people instinctively bunched closer together as they pressed forwards.

A sudden gust of air snuffed out all of the torches with a single huff. The bubble of light around them burst and the darkness flooded in. Kira stopped and the other riders bunched and bumped like a contracted caterpillar.

'Where did that wind come from?' Elian asked.

'No idea,' Kira answered. 'There's not a breath now and there wasn't any before. It was almost like someone blowing out candles. Nolita, can you ask Fire to make us some light until there's enough space for us to relight our torches, please?'

There was the slightest of pauses and then a bright orange glow with an accompanying roar from behind lit up the passageway.

'RUN!' Nolita yelled. 'Something's coming for us!'

The others did not question her. They ran. There was enough fear and urgency in her command to make them act first and ask questions later. The light dimmed briefly and then flared again. Whatever Firestorm was projecting his flame at was getting the full force of his most ferocious blast. They slowed as the blazing light faded to leave them momentarily running blind, but they kept travelling forwards, accelerating again as soon as Firestorm hurled another spraying burst of fire along the passage behind them.

Almost like punching through a wall, the riders erupted from the fog as they reached the end of the tunnel and emerged into a large underground cavern. They skidded to a momentary halt and then, realising they might possibly be trampled by their own dragons, they scattered left and right. Fang was not far behind.

In the dark of the chamber, burning red eyes looked in on them from all directions. The orange glow from Firestorm's approaching flame silhouetted outlines of six great night dragons facing them in a waiting semi-circle. As the light from Fire's flaming breath became brighter, so the waiting dragons began to close in.

Nolita screamed, the noise amplifying and multiplying as it reverberated around the huge cavern.

Firestorm exploded out from the wall of fog, his fire extinguishing before flaring back with devastating ferocity. He spewed molten fire in a broad arc to keep the approaching dragons at bay, but without effect. The night dragons continued to close in on them, apparently immune to the heat of Fire's hottest blast.

To Kira's surprise, Fang did not react to the approaching night dragons. At every other encounter with night dragons his first instinct had been to camouflage himself. This time he did nothing.

'*Is it Segun?*' she asked through the bond.

'*Relax,*' he said. '*What you are seeing is not real. They are phantoms induced by the fumes from your torches. It is only your belief that is giving them form.*'

'Can't you see them? They're all around us!' Kira persisted frantically.

'*I only see them when I look through your eyes,*' Fang said calmly. '*My sight is not so easily fooled. They are like the mist in the tunnel and the imagined movement at the edge of your vision. None of those were real. They were visions, caused by the substance you were inhaling. There is a presence here, but it feels faint like a distant echo.*'

Kira felt Fang communicating with Firestorm, but she could not hear what he said. To her horror, Fire reduced his flame to a trickle – just enough to provide a little light. Fang then walked straight towards the nearest of the approaching night dragons. It drew its head back as if to strike, mouth open wide, displaying its rows of vicious pointed teeth. Horror turned to amazement as Fang walked right through the dragon and out the other side. She blinked rapidly several times to confirm she was not seeing things.

'They're not real!' she said aloud. 'They're not real. Say it with me!' she urged the others.

'They're not real. They're . . .' she repeated the words over and over, adding volume with each repetition until she was shouting it at the top of her voice. One by one the others joined in. First Elian, then Nolita, and finally Pell began to chant the words until belief in them began to grow. All the time the night dragons closed in around them, looming larger and larger. Was it her imagination, she wondered, or were they fading?

'FORWARDS!' she yelled. Grabbing Nolita's hand again, Kira dragged her straight towards the approaching line of dragons. Nolita flinched as a night dragon lunged, closing her eyes and stumbling, but she did not stop chanting and moving forwards. One moment the dragons were there, the next they were gone. Faded into memory like a bad dream.

A glow on the far side of the chamber began almost immediately, filling the vast space with a gentle light. It looked like an amorphous cloud, much like that of the Oracle, but as it took shape it became apparent that this was not the same entity. Wings, talons and teeth – the floating vision resolved into a dragon – a dusk dragon like Fang.

'So you are here at last!' It was the same booming voice that they had heard in the hall of mirrors. It sounded pleased and relieved. 'I have waited such a long time for this day. Have you come on the Great Quest to restore the Oracle?'

'*May I have use of your mouth, Kira?*' Fang asked, his tone very formal as he made his request. Kira was surprised, but she agreed immediately.

'Yes. We have,' he said aloud.

Hearing Fang's voice coming from her mouth felt and sounded most strange. Kira was amazed that her throat could produce such a rolling, masculine voice. The others were equally astounded.

'And do you know what is needed in order for the orb to form?' the glowing apparition asked, floating down until its talons settled on the cavern floor.

It was then that Kira noticed the metal plinth, right there, next to the owner of the voice. It looked just like the one they had seen in the Valley of the Griffins.

'We do,' Fang said.

'*We do?*' she asked silently.

'*I told you I had solved the riddle,*' he told her. '*The*

297

required sacrifice will not be pleasant, but it's one I'm willing to make. This is what I was born for, Kira, but I did not want to worry you. As soon as I worked it out, I knew you would not be happy.'

'Tell me!' she ordered, her heart pounding as she tried once again to untangle the words of the rhyme.

'Your sight is true, Longfang,' the great voice announced. 'You were not deceived by the shadow demons, you saw through the mystery of the mirrors and your eyes could not be fooled by hallucinations. Step forwards then and claim the Orb of Vision. I shall remove that which is needed.'

Suddenly it all clicked into place. Kira knew what this phantom dragon was going to do and her stomach turned at the thought of it.

'No!' she cried in her mind. 'You can't do this, Fang! It's too horrible. It's wrong!'

> *Ever protected, the dusk orb lies*
> *Behind the cover, yet no disguise.*
> *Afterlife image, unreal yet real,*
> *Lives in the shadows, waits to reveal.*

An eye! The rhyme spoke of an eye! Ever protected in its socket – sometimes hidden behind its eyelid, but never disguised. Fang's eyesight was his most precious asset. He relied on his sight as much as he relied on his camouflage for protection. How could he be expected to sacrifice an eye?

This apparition in front of them must be the afterlife image. Did that make it a ghost? If so, how could it have substance enough to remove Fang's eye? Yet she knew this was exactly what it intended to do. She felt sick. What could she do to stop it?

'*You cannot stop this, Kira, so please don't try,*' Fang told her. '*I intend to see my life purpose fulfilled. You cannot take this from me.*'

'*But why does it have to be you?*' she asked. '*It was Shadow's life purpose to be killed and give her heart to form the second orb, but another dragon's heart was good enough.*'

'*It must be the eye of a dusk dragon,*' he replied. '*There are no other dusk dragons here.*'

'*There's him,*' she said, pointing at the glowing dragon next to the plinth.

'*He has no body.*' Fang's voice was sad. '*What you can see is just an echo – a shade of what he was in life.*'

'How will you take my dragon's eye?' Kira asked aloud with her own voice, choking slightly over the final two words.

Nolita gasped and the two boys looked shocked as they, too, finally grasped what was about to happen.

'There is no gentle way,' the ghostly dragon replied. 'I shall do my final duty as best I can. The Oracle has power that binds. Its purpose has held my spirit here for a long time. When my rider and I accepted the challenge to guard the plinth I had no idea I would be bound to serve beyond my physical death. I am tired. I seek the long rest of eternity that should be mine. Come. Claim the orb. It is what you are here for. You have passed the tests.'

'But you have no substance,' Kira pointed out, desperately clutching at reasons not to continue.

'I have substance enough for this one last duty,' the dragon replied. He raised his foreleg and his talons appeared to solidify.

Fang walked calmly towards the plinth and the waiting ghost dragon. Kira felt totally helpless. Fang would not listen to her. He was determined. She knew his mind. The glowing creature reached out with its scarily solid-looking talons. Kira could not watch. She turned away, ducking her head and covering her eyes with her hands, as if by protecting her own eyes she could somehow save Fang's.

'Wait!' Elian called out.

Relief made Kira feel momentarily faint. Her knees buckled under her and she fell to the ground. Tears smeared across her cheeks under her palms.

Did Elian have a way to stop this happening? She felt a hand on her back. It was Nolita's.

'Before you do this, I have some questions,' Elian continued.

The ghost dragon lowered his foreleg and regarded Elian with a chilling stare.

'Ask your questions, rider,' it said. 'But be quick. That which I have waited an age for is at hand. Do not delay my reward without reason.'

'The other orbs had perilous powers,' Elian said. 'Can you tell us what qualities this orb will possess?'

'The Orb of Vision can show you many things,' the dragon replied. 'It can show you things that are, things that have been and even things that have not yet been.'

'It has powers we can use?' Elian asked, surprised.

'The other orbs also had powers you could have wielded, if you had found the strength of will to use them. The powers are not meant for human use, though, so beware. They are fickle and there is always a price to pay for using them. Where the Orb of Vision will show you things, it will also reveal your presence to others. Do not be in a hurry to explore its power, or it may betray you.'

'The Oracle told us nothing of their powers,'

Elian said thoughtfully. 'In fact the Oracle hasn't told us a lot about anything. What do you know of the final orb?'

'Nothing.' The dragon was emphatic. 'I have no knowledge of the final orb and I want none. I just want to rest. Are your questions complete?'

'One last thing,' Elian said quickly.

Kira's heart was hammering. This was it. How could he stop the ghostly dragon from taking Fang's eye?

'I can help you to take out Longfang's eye without causing him too much pain. Will you let me help?'

'Traitor!' Kira gasped. Her head whipped round and she glared at him. She had never felt so betrayed. 'How *could* you even *think* about doing this to my dragon?'

'He won't be blinded, Kira,' Elian explained. 'He'll still be able to see with his remaining eye. It's clear he wants to do this. I know how strongly Ra feels about her life purpose. I know it's gruesome. This entire quest has been nothing like I expected. I don't want to even think about the words of the final verse. I still have to face my challenge, remember? I'm just trying to help. It will be best if I help sever the eye cleanly from the socket by using my sword and then Firestorm can heal it. This way it will be done with very little pain.'

'I don't believe this,' Kira sobbed, looking up with pleading eyes at Fang. 'Are you really going to do this?'

'Yes, Kira,' Fang replied gently. '*It's necessary. Elian's offer is kind. He does not want to see either of us in pain. Look away. Do not watch.*'

Kira knew deep down that even if she wanted to, she could not look. Turning away, she buried her head in her hands and curled up into a ball. Nolita put her arm around her and crouched by her side, also facing away from the dragons. Kira felt sick. Elian's voice had dropped to an unintelligible mutter. She reached out with her mind to Fang, but he had narrowed the bond to little more than the faintest trace in an effort to save her unnecessary pain.

'*Fang!*' She called his name with every ounce of her will, but he did not answer.

The sensation as the ghost dragon's talons eased around Fang's eyeball and into his eye socket was one that Kira would never forget. Fang was clearly trying to restrict her access to his mind, but their bond was stronger than his will. Her left eye hurt in sympathy with Fang's and, as the ghost dragon's talons probed and squeezed, it felt as if her own eye would explode.

Kira heard a loud sucking *plop* and the chamber

303

spun under her. The sudden disorientation as Fang's sight became confused, was frightening. For a moment she could see both the cavern floor and the ghost dragon in her mind's eye. Interpreting the jumbled blend of images was impossible but she did not need to open her eyes to know what was happening. Her link with Fang and her imagination gave her more than enough information. Her left eye socket suddenly felt very cold.

There was a faint swishing noise followed by a swift spike of pain. She cried out at the shock of it, clamping her hand even more firmly over her left eye and curling her body even tighter. She could feel Nolita's comforting arm around her shoulders. It felt good to have someone hold her. She had never thought to see the day when she would look to Nolita for support.

It took a moment to notice the change. A gentle breathy rumble preceded a warm glowing feeling around the left side of her head. Kira opened her eyes and stared at her knees. The flicker of Firestorm's healing blue flames gave an unearthly feel to the chamber. The confused and disturbing double image in her mind was gone. In its place was a sensation that left her more disoriented than ever. Although she could see her knees perfectly well through both of her eyes, she felt dizzy. It was as if a part of her vision were missing, yet she had never consciously 'seen' through Fang's eyes. Tears flowed in a steady stream down her cheeks, dripping to splash across her knees. She could barely feel Fang's touch. He had narrowed the bond to the finest of mental threads, but try as he might, he could not cut her off completely.

'Help me, Pell.' Elian sounded as if he were struggling with a great weight. Still she could not look.

'Balance it!'

'You can let it go now.' The booming voice of the ghost dragon sounded more distant. 'It will not fall. The plinth will do its job. You have done well.'

Kira could not look up. The tears would not stop flowing. Time had no meaning. How long had she been curled up, waiting? The light in the cavern had dimmed to almost total darkness and then increased again glowing with a steady amber light that did not have the flickering quality of Firestorm's breath. Her knees were wet with tears.

'It is over, Kira. Get up. Come and look. The orb is remarkable.'

Fang's voice was gentle in her mind. Her first instinct was to reach through the bond, but her mind recoiled from the sensation. It was not through pain, for there was none. It was the strange sympathetic sensation of hollowness that she felt in her own left eye. Without thinking she reached up to make sure it was still there.

'Ow!' It was.

Kira knew she had to face her dragon. She felt sick to the pit of her stomach, but there was no escaping it. His eye was gone.

With slow, deliberate movements, Kira rose to her feet and turned. Despite her care, she staggered. The chamber floor appeared to be trying to tip her from her feet.

'It's all right. I've got you,' Nolita said, her arm lending more than moral support.

Kira was grateful, but she could not voice her thanks. Although her first intention was to turn and look at Fang, her eyes were drawn to the rich amber glow emanating from the orb resting on the top of the metal plinth in the centre of the chamber. It was the most beautiful thing she had ever seen. It literally took her breath away. For a moment she stood, transfixed.

'*Incredible, isn't it?*' Fang said, his pride undeniable.

'Amazing!' Kira replied aloud. And she meant it. She looked up at Fang. He looked back at her through his right eye. His left eyelid was drawn down over his empty eye socket. She did not know if he was holding it closed, or if Firestorm had sealed it that way.

It did not look as bad as she had imagined, but she knew that without his second eye, Fang would never have a true sense of perspective and distance again. He would adapt, of course, but he would be vulnerable from the left side. Although there was nothing wrong with her eyes, her mind was struggling to overcome the disorientation she was feeling.

Anger flared inside her as she struggled to keep her balance. How dare Fang make this unilateral decision to let his eye be taken? When they had first met, he had been quick to tell her they were one – joined from the moment she had been born. Yet today he had been quick to sacrifice his eye – which would inevitably limit them as a team. It was never a good thing for a hunter to have a weak spot – especially such an obvious one. Fang's choice had handicapped them both.

She could not keep the icy edge from her voice as she asked him, 'Can you still sense anything through it?' She pointed at the orb.

'No,' he said, without the faintest note of apology. '*Any link I had with it was severed for ever the moment Elian cut it free. If I think at the orb I sense power, but it is not any sort of power I have ever felt before. Can you take it from the plinth? It is time we left.'*

Kira walked step by shaky step towards the orb. Nolita walked with her. As Kira approached the plinth, she found her anger replaced first by curiosity and then by a sense of awe. This orb was no larger than either of the others and yet that seemed impossible. Fang's eye had been enormous. How had it shrunk to this size? The two boys were already standing next to it, lost in wonder.

As the girls neared the orb, the light emanating from it intensified. Not in a dazzling way. Rather it grew warmer and more accepting. Kira walked right up to the plinth and reached out with both hands to lift the orb. The instant her fingertips made contact, she leaped back as if burned.

Nolita staggered as she struggled to prevent Kira from falling backwards.

'What happened?' Elian asked quickly.

'Did it hurt you?' Pell asked at the same time.

'No, it didn't hurt,' Kira replied, her voice slow, deliberate, and full of curiosity. 'The sensation was ... unexpected. The moment I touched the orb I saw Segun on Widewing. They were flying away from the castle. I pulled back through surprise. If this was a true vision, we will not have to worry about him when we leave.'

'Touch it again,' urged Pell. 'See if it confirms what you saw.'

'I wouldn't be so quick . . .' Elian began, but Kira was already moving forwards again. The flash of godlike power it had given her was irresistible. Her anger at Fang was momentarily forgotten. She reached out and placed her fingertips on the orb. This time she did not pull away.

'Yes,' she confirmed. 'He's definitely gone. It appears he has the good sense to know when to retreat. There is a problem, though. We have what we came for, but we're not going to get the orb away from here without a fight. The dragonhunters are back.'

Here ends Book Three of the Dragon Orb Quartet. Read the breathtaking climax in *Dragon Orb – Aurora.*

www.markrobsonauthor.com

FOUR DRAGONRIDERS ON A MISSION TO SAVE THEIR WORLD

FIRESTORM
Book 1 in the fantasy series.

Nolita is terrified of dragons! Learning to fly her day dragon is dangerous enough without irrational fears to contend with and a vicious dragonhunter on her tail. With Elian, another novice rider, she seeks the first of four orbs, to save the leader of all dragonkind. To do so, she must face her worst fears, and face them alone . . .

ISBN: 978-1-84738-068-5

SHADOW
Book 2 in the fantasy series.

Pell and his night dragon Shadow must find the dark orb to help save the Oracle, leader of all dragonkind. But Segun, a power-hungry tyrant, stands in their way. Pell must use his flying skills, bravery and resourcefulness to the limit, as Segun is determined to get the orb - even if it means killing the opposition.

ISBN 978-1-84738-069-2

DRAGON ORB: AURORA

Book 4 in the fantasy series.

Elian and his dawn dragon, Aurora, lead the search for the fourth
and final orb. Pursued by night dragons and helped by a WWI
airman, the four dragonriders are drawn into a huge aerial battle
between all the dragon enclaves. The ultimate fate of dragonkind
hangs by a thread. To restore order, a terrible price must be paid . . .

ISBN 978-1-84738-448-5